PINCH OF SASS

DIRE WOLF MATES
BOOK THREE

C.D. GORRI

Pinch of Sass:
Dire Wolf Mates 3
by C.D. Gorri
Edited by BookNookNuts

For Jason, Franciszka, and Flo,
you three give me so much support, I am eternally grateful!
Xoxo, C.D.

Before you begin sign up for my newsletter here:
SUBSCRIBE HERE

BLURB

Will this stoic Dire Wolf admit the sassy feline is his fated mate and stake his claim?

Ariella Golden needs to persuade sexy Dire Wolf Beta, and the amazingly talented chef at Serious Moonlight, Brock Laurent to use her Pride's corporation, Eat Well Live Proud, for all the roadhouse's needs in order to win her company's coveted quarterly prize.

But that's not the only reason this Golden girl is chasing this grumpy Wolf!

EWLP offers the best organic, non-GMO, and responsibly harvested fish and meat—going with them is a no brainer. The problem is the stubborn lil' doggy happens to be her fated mate, but he's in denial! Can the Lioness break down his barriers or will she get hurt in the process?

Brock is perfectly content to cook good food, listen to classic rock, and hang out with his Pack at their new place in Blue Valley, New Jersey. Settling down is hard on his animal, but so far so good—except for the fact he's being hunted by a pesky she-Cat.

Can't this female take a hint? He is better off alone, but this curvy, curly-headed goddess is all he thinks about lately.

Trying to ignore the pull of his mate is a losing battle. Desperate, Brock develops a plan to test whether the virginal hellcat can handle all of him. It's time to confront his fears.

Here, kitty kitty.

Stunned when Brock propositions her, but with the encouragement of her family, Ariella agrees to a single night in the sexy Dire Wolf's arms to seal the deal that will put her in the running for EWLP's quarterly prize, but that's not all. One night is all she has to get the big dumb chef to realize Ariella is exactly who the Fates designed for him.

One mate custom made with curves galore and a pinch of sass.

Will she prove she can take anything the Wolf man dishes out?

PROLOGUE

T he evening breeze was cool and sweet as Brock stood surveying the lot behind the busy commercial kitchen he now oversaw. He'd spent years cooking and mastering the finer of the culinary arts, but he rarely had a chance to practice his skill on the road.

Being part owner of the Dire Wolf MC's new roadhouse meant he was also head chef. It was a dream come true. But as with most dreams, it had its drawbacks. Like his loud as fuck Pack mate, who was right about to intrude on what was a rare moment of silence before Brock finished his shift for the night.

"Yo, Brock," Phoenix called as he walked around back.

Serious Moonlight was large for New Jersey road-house. One of a kind, really. The Dire Wolf MC had recently purchased, renovated, and now the restaurant/bar that sat on the outskirts of Blue Valley. Life was different now. They'd all parked their motorcycles for good and were trying their hand at making this their real home.

Each member of the Pack had something he or she handled and excelled at. Derreck was the Alpha and ran just about everything, including money stuffs, paperwork, and permits. Phoenix was their resident mechanic. Brock the head chef. But they all pitched in at the bar.

Between that and the occasional weekend road trip, Brock could safely say he was pretty fond of life right now. Or he would be if everyone could remember he was the Pack Beta, second to the Alpha, and deserving of some damn privacy.

"Brock? Where are you, man? Moody fucker," Phoenix mumbled, and Brock bit back his snarl.

He might be a genius when it came to cooking, but he had zero tolerance for interruptions of any kind, especially when he was working. Phoenix's caterwauling was a motherfuckin' interruption.

"Dammit, Brock," Phoenix continued to yell. "I appreciate that sometimes a man needs a bit of quiet, and I hated to intrude," said with more than a little snark, "but I need your signature in this EWLP purchase order, for fuck's sake!"

Brock frowned. He knew when Sheila had insisted, they start ordering meat from the local Lion Pride's corporation, *Eat Well Live Proud,* that shit was going to get fucked up. Just because she was mated to one of those big, fussy-haired pussies didn't mean Brock had to jump when they snapped.

That was not saying he was not glad for the change. Brock would be the first to admit that *EWLP* offered the best organically fed and environmentally conscious raised beef, pork, lamb, and fowl he'd ever tasted. He hardly minded singing their praises, even if it meant giving props to the feline run firm. Word was their fish was decent, too. He just hadn't gotten around to ordering some.

Time really flew when you were busy making a home. Even now, he could hardly believe it was almost ten o'clock at night. Where had the day gone?

Brock scratched his head, heaved out a sigh. He was still ignoring his Pack mate, fucking Phoenix was totally cold, checking for Brock near the woods that bordered their land.

He wondered if time was going to keep moving this quickly since they'd parked their bikes for good.

Life was different now. Derrick and Sheila had both found mates, but that kind of thing was not in his future.

"Brock? The fuck, man!" Phoenix yelled, still looking for him, and it was actually kind of embarrassing at this point.

Couldn't the man scent him? Even without using that sense, couldn't he see the enormous blond Dire Wolf Shifter that Brock was standing not four yards away from him? He just had to look around the empty crates stacked neatly against the back wall. He'd have to tell Derrick the Pack needed to spend some time re-training their senses.

Yep, shit was weird now. Brock hardly recognized them anymore, and that wasn't necessarily a bad thing. The Dire Wolf MC he grew up in simply didn't exist. Each of his Pack mates had willingly turned their backs on their nomadic heritage when they bought this land and opened up shop.

Even the Alpha's dam, who rode with her own MC of widowed and single she-Wolves, could hardly imagine them running a roadhouse bar and grill. She'd visited just last month to meet her son's mate and to congratulate them on the coming birth of their first cub. Derrick had picked good when he found Lucy.

Brock admired the spunky little feline and did his damndest to stay on her good side. Hell, even if he pissed her off, he could always bribe her with the double chocolate caramel brownies she could not get enough of in her fertile state. Sometimes, it really paid to be a chef.

Business was good. Everyone was happy. Well, *sort of.* Even Phoenix seemed to appreciate having time to devote to exploring ways to renovate and improve the custom modifications he made to cars and motorcycles for Shifters and other supernaturals. Human machinery just couldn't handle the wear and tear of lugging around a man who harbored an eight hundred pound monster inside of him. He'd even started selling them.

Good for Phoenix.

But honestly, Brock was content. Thanks to their Alpha's business savvy and his mate's grit, Sheila's badass attitude and marketing skills, they had a good thing going here.

He ran a hand through his dark blond hair and shook it out before he re-tied the plain black headband he wore to keep it out of the way while he cooked. Normally, Brock hated shit in his hair, but when he was in the kitchen, safety and health precautions took precedence over personal style preferences.

His Dire Wolf pressed against his skin, the beast agitated. That was nothing new. He'd felt that way for months now. He rubbed his chest and closed his eyes, wrestling with his inner animal until the Wolf was calm once more.

Shit.

That was close. He would have to go for a run later. Brock was just so unfocused lately. Hardly his fault, he thought, narrowing his eyes. Ever since Sheila had come back home with her very own Lion Prince mate, the roadhouse had been crawling with the pesky felines.

Fucking furballs were everywhere. Of course, Brock didn't usually get riled up because of one Shifter group or other. He wasn't a speciesist. He just wanted to be alone sometimes. Was that too much to ask for?

As a rare and prehistoric species of Shifter, Dire Wolves were often more dominant and growly than most. Very few Shifters could match their inherent size and strength, which was why his kind typically roamed. Challenges were a Shifter's way of life, but not theirs. Dire Wolves were basically pacifists, separating them from other, more instinct-run Shifters.

His objections to the feline furballs were really reserved for one spectacularly sassy feline in particular. And the reason behind that was so shameful, so twisted, so damned embarrassing, he could hardly admit it to himself.

But what else could Brock do? Ariella Golden haunted his every waking—and sleeping—hour. She was temptation personified. A woman custom built to suit his tastes by the gods themselves.

Fucking hell.

The woman had him waxing poetic over something that had everything to do with hormones and nothing at all to do with deities. It was just a fluke of nature. A Biological imperative created to ensure the propagation of the species. Nothing else. Nothing special.

Keep telling yourself that, bro.

So, what if her skin reminded him of freshly rendered cream? And if her hair was deep and rich like his favorite espresso beans? That didn't mean shit. Who cared if her full lips and golden eyes made him wish for things he hadn't dared long for since he was a pup?

She was nothing to him. Nothing at all.

Even as he thought it, he felt the lie burn his soul. His Dire Wolf pressed once more, the beast letting him feel his rage with a snarling snap of his jaws that made Brock's own head ache like hell.

Fuck.

He might as well admit it, if only in his head.

Ariella Golden was his fated mate.

CHAPTER 1

Knowing you had a fated mate, and claiming said mate, were two entirely different things. Especially for him. Brock was not built for a mate.

Period.

Sure, Ariella Golden was the one woman the universe had destined to be his. Unfortunately, the universe had fucked up. He had no plans to take her, claim her, fuck her until his mind went blank and his body was finally sated.

Grrrr. What a visual!

Whatever. He couldn't do a thing about it. So Brock had been avoiding her like the plague. Ever since the first time he'd taken the curvy female for a ride on the back of his Harley, Brock had been trying to fight it. Even now, memories of that ride had his dick growing hard in his pants.

He could almost feel her as she'd been that day. The woman had squeezed him so tight, she damn near busted a rib. But it would have been worth it. The feel of her tits smashed against his back, her hot womanly core snuggled up to his hips, had made him feel ten times a man.

He suspected her Lioness had scented what they were to each other. Brock had seen the shocked glee sparkling in her golden gaze as she'd looked up at him in the smoky, dim light of the bar later that very same night.

But like a fucking idiot and worse, a coward, he'd turned around and walked out. Ever since, he'd been pretending not to notice her. Hell. Ignoring Ariella was the hardest fucking thing he'd ever done, but he'd been pulling it off for months now.

Brock had choked big time, and now he didn't know what to do. It was stupid, really. A bad memory from the past was killing his future, but the truth was he didn't know if he could handle another rejection. That's why he decided to stay away.

Like a fucking coward.

His Wolf growled, and he rubbed his chest to

quiet the beast. He didn't like being called a coward, but what else was it when you ran from the woman the fates decided was yours? Not like she took the hint anyway, he thought with a shake of his head.

Ariella Golden had made it her business to visit *Serious Moonlight* with increased frequency. Which, of course, only made things harder on him.

Literally.

She had him so out of his mind Brock was snapping at everyone lately. Cursed more, too. And he'd been walking around with a fucking bat in his jeans, trying to run the kitchen staff as if no one could tell. He was fighting with his Pack mates, and himself. His Wolf wanted to kick his own ass.

Derrick had called him into his office three times this week. Lucy, his pregnant mate, had developed a nose for romantic schemes and Brock wanted no part of it. She'd even threatened him with some magical matchmaking nonsense.

Slick one, that Lucy. When she wasn't trying to fix up members of the Pack, she was making them move the heavy, wood furniture she'd had them refinish, from room to room for no specific reason at all. Just whenever she got the notion. Which seemed to be constantly, the last few weeks.

Derrick had simply smiled at his mate like the

lovesick fool he was and called it her nesting period, which to a Dire Wolf made no fucking sense, whatsoever. They weren't birds, for fuck's sake. True, Lucy was a feline, but as far as Brock knew, they didn't have nests either.

Then again, who was he to judge? Brock was outside in the dark because—*let's face it*—he was hiding. Him. A badass Dire Wolf Shifter. Beta to the Pack. And head chef at *Serious Moonlight*. Hiding.

The shame!

He'd known the moment Ariella had walked into the roadhouse that night. He had felt it in the air. The woman caused the very electricity in the atmosphere to alter whenever she appeared.

It was the same damn thing every single time the female entered any room near his immediate vicinity. And yet, he was still too weak to do a thing about it.

Echoes of past wounds still hurt, despite his denials. Brock wasn't sure he could take a chance on being spurned again. Not with Ariella. He couldn't risk it. Something inside told him he would never survive if that golden-eyed beauty rejected him. Admitting that one solitary fear made his entire body tremble with emotion.

Shameful. Weak. Alone. Always alone.

He growled and cursed himself ten times a fool. Brock froze when, at that moment, the sounds of her laughter reached him as the bar's side door swung open. He closed his eyes, gritting his teeth at the tidal wave of lust that damn near bowled him over.

He still wasn't prepared for the fierce punch of desire that slammed into him, hitting him right in the gut whenever he caught sight, sound, or scent of her. His Wolf growled, pulse raced, and fuck, he was sweating.

Yes, it was all because a certain sexy siren had walked into the bar looking like heaven and smelling like sin. Brock's Wolf had been growling nonstop ever since. He'd just cooked her meal and sent it out with their best server. Then, he hightailed it out the back door. He just had to escape, get away from her moans and groans as she enjoyed her dinner.

Ariella was very vocal when it came to her enjoyment. Satisfaction flashed through him as he pictured her eating the food, he had made just for her. Of course, that was followed by another pang of carnal lust so strong he doubled over and had to readjust his cock inside his chef's pants.

He'd never worn the things until she started

coming to the bar to eat every other day, but jeans were simply too constrictive. At least, this way, he wouldn't punch a hole through the baggy material with his stone hard dick.

And wasn't that the source of all his issues?

Most guys would be giddy as all hell with a cock that size, but Brock knew better. Being big wasn't all it was cracked up to be. Sometimes, it was downright fucking tough. Females were not as fond of size as they implied. Especially inexperienced females.

Brock couldn't stomach the idea she might be afraid of him in bed. And it was not something he relished finding out.

The door swung shut again, and with it went the sound of her voice. Thank fuck. He was glad she was enjoying the food, but for fuck's sake, the sound of her moans was almost unbearable.

Mine, growled his Dire Wolf, his animal scratching hard against his skin.

It was difficult to wrestle for control, but he managed it, promising the monster a good long run later that night. It was all he could do to stop himself from hunting her down and rutting her like a beast.

We are a beast, the animal returned, and not as if it were a bad thing.

Brock growled deep in his throat as he wrestled for calm. He wasn't a self-hating Shifter. Not exactly. He just happened to have a past. Didn't everyone? It would be better for them both if she simply moved on.

Vexing female. Stubborn beauty.

He should just leave when she came in. But he didn't. His Wolf would not let him.

Possessive monster.

In fact, he was the only one who handled her food when she came into the bar. No one else touched Ariella's plate. Not ever. It was an unwritten rule in the kitchen and the entire staff understood and steered clear.

Well, duh.

His Wolf growled, the animal seeming to roll his eyes from inside that plane of existence where he waited for Brock to call on his furry form. His staff wasn't stupid. Almost all of them were Shifters, and they knew what was up.

Especially after he'd tossed the former sous chef out the back door, head over teakettle, for adjusting the amount of sauce on Ariella's grilled *mahi-mahi* a few weeks ago. No one had made that mistake again.

Mine, growled his Wolf, and Brock rubbed his chest harder this time.

His keen ears picked up the sound of Phoenix. The fucker was finally rounding the right corner to find Brock's little hiding spot. He braced himself for the intrusion.

"Hey, bro, I've been looking for you," his Pack mate said and grinned. In his hand, he held a tablet and a stylus. The prick didn't even look pissed he'd been walking around ten minutes trying to find Brock. Lucky fucker, having no worries.

"You gotta sign this, bro."

"Thanks," Brock grumbled and scribbled his signature on the order.

They'd been slowly transitioning all their needs from various butchers and fishmongers to *Eat Well Live Proud*. It wasn't for any other reason than the fact the Lions delivered a superior product—*organic, non-GMO, and sustainably harvested.*

Win-win.

Truth was, Shifters had refined palates. Some of the other supernatural species as well. They really appreciated the finer quality of the meat, game, and fish EWLP offered. Derrick left the kitchen up to him, so it was completely his choice, and yet he'd delayed in switching their entire line of produce, meat, and fish to the feline run corp.

Some would say it was because he was still undecided about what to do with his unclaimed mate. Of course, should those people voice this opinion out loud, they would find themselves following his former sous chef out the back door, ass over teakettle, as it were.

"So, Ariella's inside," Phoenix idiotically pointed out.

"Yes," Brock answered while he read over the order.

"And you're out here?"

"Your point exactly?" Brock growled.

"Nothin' bro. Just sayin' because, you know, her mom's in there, and if I didn't know any better, I would say Aunt Patty's got a vial of catnip up her sleeve," Phoenix muttered.

The casual reference was to the only herbal supplement that had the power to act like a drug in the systems of feline Shifters. Brock's head shot up. Patricia Golden was the most shockingly carefree, potentially dangerous, feline over sixty Brock had ever met. The woman was a party animal. And she was not above involving her daughters in whatever hairbrained scheme she thought of next. Lucky for her son, he was too much of a stuffed shirt to become entangled in her wild affairs.

On the other hand, Ariella—*sweet, beautiful, inno-*

cent, and probably frustrated as hell if she felt anything like he did—Ariella was just ripe for the picking. Brock closed his eyes and tried to rein in his beast. Patricia Golden was inside *Serious Moonlight* right now, possibly dosing her daughter with the one substance as close to a narcotic as it got for cat Shifters.

Oh, for fuck's sake.

"Well, you know the mess she caused after the last time that ol' Lioness pulled a stunt like this," Phoenix continued, rubbing his hand on the back of his neck.

Brock immediately thought of the incident a few weeks ago when that cunning older Lioness had spiked all the kegs under the bar with *Magibrew* enhancer, a special potion made by Witches that could slow Shifter metabolism when applied to alcohol, getting them just as knackered as normals.

"Anyway, bro, I thought I'd give you a heads up," Phoenix ended his muddled up explanation and wisely took a step back.

This was not good. If Brock remembered correctly—and he did, while under the effects of the *Magibrew* every Shifter in the bar had gotten drunk as hell. Drunk Shifters meant fistfights, and that meant they'd had broken bottles, barstools, a few tables, and one window to replace afterwards. Not to mention having to turn the hose on their customers because of all the outdoor fucking that had gone on.

Lucy had even made them sanitize the entire outdoor parking lot with a pressure washer and outdoor bleach, the commercial kind. It had been a total shitshow, and he was not looking forward to a repeat.

Of course, he'd also learned something interesting during that night. When drunk, naïve little Ariella was not only extremely agreeable, but she was also somewhat prone to falling asleep. Which is how he'd found her, passed out with a smile on her lips in the bed of a pickup truck with two Bear Shifters who'd been about to cart her off to their hometown to mate her.

Brock had nearly Wolfed out and killed both those fuckers. Luckily, Derrick had saved him from manslaughter and talked the drunk Bears out of it. Offering them a case of honey mead to take home in exchange for the Lioness. Brock had carried her to the Pack House, where she'd slept it off in his room.

He'd had to stay in Wolf form, outside his

bedroom window where she slept it off for the dura-tion of the night, otherwise he might have claimed her himself.

"How did she get it inside past Thor?" Brock asked his Pack mate.

"Don't know. Maybe she hid it?"

Fuck.

Patricia was always trying to get their Enforcer to search her. Crazy flirtatious woman. She needed a mate to settle her, but Brock didn't think any of the Dire Wolves were it for the Golden matriarch. Hell, the woman needed a keeper. Putting her daughter in harm's way, she should be ashamed of herself! And Brock should have his head examined.

What did he care? He was not taking the younger Golden as his mate, so what did it matter if one Bear or two took her home?

Fuck that. Of course, it mattered. His Wolf almost ripped out of his skin at the mere thought. How did he ever get entangled in this mess, anyway?

"You know, this is all Sheila's fault. Ever since she mated Leo, this place has been crawling with crazy felines," Phoenix muttered, and Brock had to agree.

And he liked Leo! But why did Sheila have to adopt his totally inappropriate and possibly insane extended family and bring them here?

Fuck. Fuck. FUCK.

"I'm gonna ban that woman," Brock growled, grabbing his cell phone.

He started texting the rest of the DWMC, alerting them of Patricia's shenanigans. It was all fun and games till someone got kidnapped and forced into a mating with two Bears! Brock growled even louder at the thought.

"I mean, Patricia Golden is one spunky Lioness, but I don't think she means any harm," Phoenix said.

Phoenix was right to a point, Brock conceded. The Golden matriarch simply had a penchant for trouble. Sure, they all lovingly referred to her as Aunt Patricia, but Brock strongly felt the woman had a responsibility to Ariella she was negating.

At the very least, she had some very unusual ideas about what constituted proper mother-daughter outings. Like the strip show she'd taken Ariella, Sheila, and Lucy to last week. She'd claimed it was a ballet, but when Derrick had thought to surprise his mate, he'd found her waving dollar bills and laughing her ass off while a group of men danced on poles in nothing but banana hammocks.

"I mean, Derrick is still pissed about the strip show," Phoenix added.

"As our Alpha has every right to be, Phoenix, and you know it."

"Come on. I mean, did he really have to scoop Lucy up and carry her out to his new Suburban? They argued loudly and made up even more loudly. The moans and rocking of that big ass SUV about scarred me for life! Do you know I had to stand guard and listen to that? Gross, bro! Like hearing your parents fuck," Phoenix mumbled, his cheeks turning beet red.

Brock shuddered at the imagery. Gross. He'd been desperately trying to forget that whole incident for days now. Phoenix was right about one thing. That little anecdote had all the charm of hearing your parents having sex, and Brock was dutifully grossed out by it.

He'd been there too and had quietly convinced the other ladies to let him drive them home. They'd agreed, but only after "Aunt" Patricia stuck a hundred-dollar bill into the g-string of one extremely oiled up dancer. She'd insisted on tucking it right between his cheeks.

Ouch.

Even his Wolf cringed at the recollection. Dammit. If she was here and had a vial of catnip, it could only spell trouble. The question was, for who?

His cell phone buzzed, and Brock answered it curtly. It was Sheila confirming what Phoenix had just said. Ariella was at the mercy of her crazy mother and a damn vial of catnip. If he didn't move his ass, who knew what would happen?

Grrr.

CHAPTER 2

Meanwhile...

"OH MY GAWD!"

Ariella Golden moaned loudly and slammed her hands on the uncovered wood table of her favorite new Blue Valley haunt. She was in the throes of culinary ecstasy.

"Yes. Yes. YES!" she cried out like Meg Ryan in that famous movie scene.

The salmon sashimi appetizer with slices of fresh avocado, wasabi ginger sauce, and little fried wontons on the side—necessary bits of deliciousness used to scoop up the plump pieces of fish—was possibly the best damn thing she had ever eaten.

If the place wasn't already famous for the generous drink menu, featuring locally brewed IPAs and artisan liquors, kickass live music, and the over-the-top gorgeous owners, *Serious Moonlight* would be a hit for the food alone.

The establishment was still fairly new to town and, as far as the normals new, it was owned and operated by an ex-motorcycle club. She knew better, of course. Being a Shifter and all. The Dire Wolf Motorcycle Club might be retired, but the badass prehistoric Shifters still liked to ride. She'd even been on the back of one of their bike's once—the memory replaying in her head like a favorite reel on social media.

The DWMC had only recently moved to Blue Valley, New Jersey, buying this property and settling down for the first time in their history. But that wasn't the reason she dined there three times a week, minimum. The truth was, Ariella just couldn't stay away.

Despite the constant disregard he'd shown her, her Lioness was stuck on the Pack Beta. Silly kitty insisted Brock Laurent, head chef and sexy as fuck Dire Wolf, was her fated mate.

Prrrr.

Oh, she had it bad. Feeding her lonely heart on the mere fact he was near to her whenever she ate at the rustically charming roadhouse had been her only recourse. Ever since that one fateful ride where she'd scented his masculine musk and fur, she'd known he was hers. But he didn't feel the same, as evidenced by his hasty withdrawal and ghost act.

Sigh.

So, eating out became her go to. Maybe she could catch him off guard, wear him down or something. Then maybe his beast would choose her as surely as hers had chosen him—*if only.*

Hell, she would go every single day if she thought it might help. But then he might catch on to her plan. Not that she had a plan, but she was working up to one. Ariella didn't want the man to assume the worst about her. Like the fact she was little better than a stalker.

Double sigh.

But what was she supposed to do? Ariella tried to forget about him by throwing herself into work, but every night when she lay alone in her bed, there he was, big and blond and larger than life, playing inside her brain like her own personal home movie.

Unfortunately, every attempt she'd made to discuss their possible fated mate status, or any rela-tionship at all, had ended with a curt glare and him walking away. Sure, she hated to see him leave, but she loved watching him go. That boy filled out a pair of jeans better than she did.

It was getting old, though. The whole thing where she tried to talk, and he gave her dirty looks and ran away. Ariella hardly ever got a word out past his name. He was always growling and angry at her no matter what she did—and he never, ever listened!

Ugh.

Bad qualities for a mate. Really. And yet, he was everything she ever wanted. Ariella had even started doubting whether her Lioness was right about the whole fated mate thing. Maybe it was just a stupid crush. She had been guilty of that a time or two, but she never thought any of them were her one and only. Maybe it was just a stupid myth, like some Shifters believed.

Rrrrrrawr.

Her she-Cat roared as she always did whenever Ariella doubted herself. Her feisty feline was spunky and honest in ways her human side still feared. Ariella readily embraced that side of herself, knowing full well the big kitty was a big ol' toughie on the outside and had a heart softer than a kitten's fur on the inside.

"How is everything tonight?" a passing server asked.

Her dinner date—*her baby brother George*—nodded politely, his brown eyes wide as he stared at the pretty young waitress. He was even worse than Ariella when it came to dating. Poor guy. But he was just so much fun to razz!

"Tell the chef it would be even better if he used higher quality fish," Ariella responded and smirked at the sudden paleness of her face.

No one wanted to confront Brock with a comment like that.

"She's kidding. It was great," George said, covering Ariella's mouth and nodding at the poor girl.

"Oh, that's funny. Ha ha," the server mumbled, walking away.

"What is wrong with you? You wanna get her fired?" George scolded.

"I was only teasing, but George, you know EWLP has better stock," she shrugged.

"I swear you are getting nuttier by the day, Ariella," her brother replied, heaving a sigh as he went back to his smart phone.

As the King's new personal assistant, George Golden had his hands full. What a stuffed shirt her brother was! Couldn't even relax for an evening meal. He was alright, for a boy, but she wished one of her sisters had been free this evening. Toni was busy with some spreadsheets, and Annabeth was busy spreading beneath the sheets with her new mate.

Hmmm. Maybe she should have gone the matchmaker route too? Oh well. Too late now. She already knew who her fated mate was. He just wasn't into her.

Sad prrrr.

"So, give me some Pride gossip, *Georgie Porgie,*" Ariella said, using the nickname he hated.

"You live in the Pride community, Ariella," he grumbled.

"Yeah, but I'm not inside the Palace, like you. What's going on with King Donovan and Mom, anyway?"

Donovan Crowley was King of the Blue Valley Pride. He'd been poisoned by his trusted valet for months before his son, the prince, Detective Leo Crowley, and his mate, Dire Wolf Shifter, Sheila Rand, discovered the matter and solved it promptly.

Ariella's mother, Patricia, was the king's late wife's best friend. She'd stayed inside the Palace after those horrible events to nurse King Donovan back to health. But something had happened, and she'd hightailed it out of there like her tail was on fire.

Always up for a party, something was off with their mom lately, and that rat George knew about it, she was sure. Patricia was behaving wilder than usual.

"I am not privy to the King's private affairs, and even if I were, I would not discuss them with you," George replied, ignoring her.

Ariella snarled and pinched him beneath the table. Satisfied she hurt him enough after George yelped like a cub, Ariella's thoughts drifted back to Brock.

Again.

She was usually shy with men but being ignored had turned her into the aggressor. That was a new experience, for sure. Furthermore, it was not something she particularly liked.

Frowning, she thought about the past few months. Work was always a good outlet for amped up nerves, and she'd been killing it at *EWLP*. Ever since Brock Laurent had all but rejected her, she'd thrown herself into work.

Ariella had gone after every unclaimed account in the region to add to their client list. Her boss had even announced she had single-handedly made *Eat Well Live Proud* the biggest sustainably harvested seafood distributor in the area. It made sense since most of the other reps seemed to concentrate on their meat products to boost numbers. Fish was a tougher sell, but Ariella had grit and determination on her side.

She achieved her goals by securing entire bulk orders for many of the smaller, top quality, but lesser known high end food stores, restaurants, and catering businesses across Blue Valley, and the neighboring towns of Maccon City, Barvale, Northern, East Cove, Daniels' Bay, Maverick Point, and the little known town of Castor's Corner. Signing several small accounts at once was the same as landing any big hotel chain, and she was on the track to hunt down the regional manager of Stein Luxury Resorts—if she could only find out who he or she was!

Serious Moonlight was another hold out. Yes, they ordered most of their meat and had sampled fish from *EWLP*, but they'd yet to go exclusively with the feline firm. And that was what she was after —exclusivity.

Ariella still firmly believed small business was where she would get the most for her efforts. It was her unique one-on-one approach that had gotten her this far. Where most of the others in her department had four or five large clients, Ariella now had a hundred and seventy accounts up and down the East Coast, most in New Jersey.

She worked harder than anyone she knew, but that was okay. Ariella enjoyed the challenge and the claim that she now had the most accounts accrued in a single quarter. If she were lucky, she would also boast the most revenue earned out of all her Pride mates at the corporation once the quarter ended.

That particular contest was something of a big deal since the winner got an all-expense-paid-two-week-vacation to Moongate Island. The exclusive resorts located there had special suites catering to the supernatural crowd. Ariella had always wanted to go. In fact, their website had been bookmarked repeatedly. It was the one destination where she placed all her romantic fantasies.

Sigh.

The honeymoon of her dreams existed some-where on that island. She'd been picturing it since she was a cub. Images of a big strong man who could handle her Lioness' curves and less than gracious exuberance with ease and diplomacy. A man who wanted and loved her. She used to imagine herself mated to a big Lion male, but lately it was a Dire Wolf haunting her dreams.

A tall, blond, sexy Dire Wolf Shifter, with a

wicked grin and a body she couldn't wait to explore. A man who wanted her, appreciated her, and was willing to be equal partners in a mating that mattered. Someone who knew his way around the kitchen, who would hand feed her delicious island delicacies in between bouts of erotic lovemaking.

Yowza. Was it getting hot in here?

Ariella bit back her moan as naughty images of her and Brock sunbathing in the nude in a tropical paradise flashed through her brain. Okay, so it wasn't a G-rated fantasy, but it was hers, and she would not apologize for it.

Sigh.

Ariella had always imagined what would happen the day she found her mate. They'd meet, they'd kiss, and they'd live happily ever after. Okay, there was some stuff in between—like super sticky smexy fun times she was glossing over because a virgin could only imagine so much—still, that was generally how it was *supposed* to happen.

Only, it hadn't gone down like that. Not at all. Brock just didn't have the same *boom-you-are-mine* reaction she did when they met. And now, her Lioness was stuck on a male who did not want her.

Sad sad prrrrrr.

Not everyone believed in destiny, but Ari was a

dreamer. She'd spent years waiting to lavish the never ending supply of love and affection she'd been saving up since forever on some lucky male. Her fated mate. Her one and only. And yep, that wasn't all she'd been saving.

Ariella was still technically untouched—as in virginal. She'd been waiting for her special someone to come along to initiate her into the carnal arts. Oh, Ari enjoyed sexy fun times as much as the next girl, but most boys were so fragile they could hardly take getting to third base with her. Lionesses were strong as fuck. So here she was, almost thirty-years old, and she'd never done the deed with an actual male.

All the vibrators and sexy toys in the world couldn't make up for how it would feel to be claimed by her one true mate. But the stuck-up, goody-two shoes, all about himself, Chef and Beta Wolf, Brock Laurent, didn't want her.

Pfbbbbttttt.

Joking aside, it hurt like hell that he didn't feel anything for her at all. Pain at the reminder shot through her, replacing the euphoric haze she'd been in after consuming every last bite of her appetizer.

Dang it.

She hated when that happened. Maybe Mom was right. Maybe all she needed was a one-way ticket to boinktown. Then she could forget the slap of Brock's rejection. But how was that going to happen when he was the only man who made her hot and bothered?

Mate, her inner kitty growled.

Ari rolled her eyes at her inner Lioness. The traitor. All the big she-Cat wanted to do was rub herself all over the six-and-a-half foot Wolf whom she idiotically worshipped and couldn't wait to sink her teeth into. It wasn't like she hadn't given him the opportunity to give her a good, long sniff or anything during that crazy bike ride. The man had taken off with her clinging to his back like a bat out of hell down the highway on his Harley Davidson FXSTB Night Train.

Yes, she had the name of his ride memorized after he'd nearly gone apeshit when she'd referred to it as merely a bike. Okay. She was exaggerating—something Ariella did often. Brock hadn't exactly gone nuts, he'd just growled, and sniffed like she'd passed something decidedly unladylike on his precious Harley.

Whatevah.

He could just take his snobbish, standoffish behavior and stick it where the sun never shined! She couldn't abide folks who thought they were better than everyone else and judging from his attitude, that was Brock Laurent to a T.

But what did he have that she didn't besides the obvious? And wasn't that what they were supposed to have to, *er*, get a move on with things?

"Hey, what happened to your highlights?" George interrupted her train of thought.

"My hair?" she asked, bunching up her dark curls.

"Yeah. I thought you were bleaching and straightening these days," he muttered, taking a sip of his club soda.

Pussy.

"I only did that to try to blend in with Cousin Margaret for her wedding party. Those haughty beyotches always give me shit cause my hair is dark, but I decided to go back to my natural brown. Why, does it look bad?"

"No. It looks fine," George replied noncommittally. "But are you sure you aren't trying to tempt a certain Dire Wolf Shifter to glance your way? I heard Brock mention disliking fake things last time we were here," he murmured, still looking at his phone.

Ariella growled deep in her throat. George was such a fucker. He always pretended not to notice shit and then he spilled things like that. Whatever the reason she'd stopped dying her hair, it didn't matter. Ariella and Brock Laurent were at a stalemate.

"I'm over him," Ariella told her brother with feigned nonchalance.

"Are you? I thought you said he was your fated mate?"

"Yeah. I mean, I might have been wrong about that."

Like dead wrong. Her heart squeezed painfully in her chest, but that didn't change facts. Ari had to stop wasting her life and stressing over the man.

"So, what now?"

"Well, mom always says a good backscratching could solve a lot. Maybe I need a date!"

"Ariella, what are you on about?"

"Of course, that's just another euphemism for sex, George. I mean, I don't want to be an old maid. Is that still a saying?"

"What?!"

"Sex, George. I'm talking about getting laid. I need D-I-C-K."

"What the hell, Ari?! Oh my God! I do not want to have this conversation with my sister and especially not in public," George hissed, looking around like someone overheard us.

"Come on, George. Don't you have friends? Call some of them up to meet us here. Be my wingman!"

"You have lost your mind," he muttered, shaking his head.

"Mom says I have fantastic assets, which she attributes to herself, of course, but she said I could have my pick of men if I just get out there. Come on, help a girl out," she begged.

"I can't believe this. Ariella Golden, you are ruining my dinner," he grumbled.

Ari snorted with laughter. She was only half-kidding, but it was worth it just to see Georgie Porgie sweat a little. And for the record, she wasn't conceited, but she was pretty, even if she had curves on her curves.

Along with plenty of T and A, she had long legs and flawless skin, sparkling amber-colored eyes that glowed gold with her Lioness, and an awesome sense of humor, if she did say so herself. She had plenty to offer the right male.

"Want dessert after we get our entrees?" George asked, frowning at the menu.

Her brother was always hungry, and he often ate like a damn pig, but he never gained an ounce. Lucky fucker. He straightened his tie as he glared at the dance floor. There was some kind of ruckus going on, and Ariella smirked. Prim and proper was her baby bro.

Total dork.

And yet she was the last virgin standing in their family. Sometimes, life was just utterly unfair.

Grrrr.

CHAPTER 3

"Seriously, Ari, you gonna split the tomahawk steak with me?" he asked.

"No, you ate almost all of it last time, and I was starving."

"You don't look like you're starving," he muttered, and she kicked him under the table.

The band was on break, and someone put a loud dance song on. Ariella didn't mind, but she knew George hated just about anything other than rock music. She grinned and shook her head, bopping to the beat.

"Get your own dinner, dork face," she replied.

"Fine."

The server returned for their entrée orders, and Ariella tried to appear nonchalant about the whole thing. She wondered if Brock was even in the kitchen tonight. So far, she hadn't seen hide nor hair of the blond giant. George was rambling on about something, but she was too busy wallowing in self misery to pay any attention.

Stop it.

"Hello? Earth to Ari. I am talking to you. Why are we here?"

"You're the one who followed me, *Georgie Porgie*," she swallowed down another mouthful of the sumptuous white wine she'd ordered with her appetizer.

"I told you I had to drop off some legal forms to Leo, and Sheila is always my best chance of pinning that man down. You know how he is."

"Yes, Georgie, I know," she replied and bit back her laughter at her brother's annoyed expression.

It was always fun teasing her baby bro. Ari sighed and pushed her now empty plate towards the center of the table. The appetizer had been sublime. She might be pissed at Brock, but he was one hell of a chef. She continued to think so as the next course was served.

"Gimme a bite," George whined, sticking his fork in her swordfish steak.

"There's three pounds of Argentinian beef on

your plate, George, hands off my fish," she snapped at him.

Seafood was her weakness, and nothing was better than a perfectly fried Atlantic cod. The dish was almost perfect. Only one thing could make it better. Some of that good quality sustainably harvested seafood that only Eat Well Live Proud could deliver.

If only she could convince him to switch all his fish to their new eco-friendly seafood line. It was of a much better grade than what he was serving now, and this was good stuff. But she was certain she could do better for Brock, *er*, that was, for the restaurant. Not the man. He was not hers to do anything for. Or to.

Gulp.

What?

"I bet this place could take number one in *Blue Valley Monthly's* Top Ten Eateries," George said, and he wasn't wrong.

The list was posted every month like clockwork in print and on the monthly magazine's website. Who didn't want that kind of free advertising? She shook her head and took another sip of wine, emptying the glass as she contemplated the problem.

Her own palate was highly developed and where

she appreciated the seasoning and superb technique Brock used to create his dishes, the fact was this was not the best seafood available, and really, why shouldn't it be?

Taste buds still tingling with delight, Ari eyed her brother's food and, just because she could, she reached over and snagged George's still untouched side dish. She scooted it a bit closer to her side of the table, scooping the delicious creamed spinach into her mouth and moaning triumphantly at the wonderful texture and flavors.

George simply rolled his eyes and pushed it all the way in front of her.

"Go ahead, Ari. I told you, I didn't want the creamed spinach when you ordered it," he grumbled.

Ariella didn't want to overdo it, but one more bite wouldn't hurt. The creamy goodness had a hint of lemon zest on top. So good, it actually made her forget it was an actual vegetable dish.

"Well, thanks for inviting me, sis. But next time, maybe we do lunch instead," George frowned as the band came back on stage. They were tuning their instruments, and the lead singer started getting the audience hyped up with some banter.

Ariella looked on and grinned. Things were

gonna be fun tonight. She could already feel it sizzling in the air, like magic.

"I mean, Brock is a talented chef, but this place is so, so—"

"Fun?" she supplied and giggled at her stick-in-the-mud sibling's expense. "Georgie, you need to let your hair down."

He wasn't the only one. Her inner Lioness purred happily, and she patted her now full tummy with a smile on her lips. It was a fact, her would-be mate was a genius.

"Oh crap! Ari, we should go now. Mom is here," George was half turned in his chair and squinting at where a loud ruckus sounded out from across the bar.

Sure enough, Patricia Golden, their own mother, with her silver streaked hair and a pair of pleather pants that should be deemed illegal painted on her butt, was the cause of it.

It was eight o'clock on a Saturday night, and the band was just right, playing the kind of rock and roll music that made you want to dance and fuck and fight maybe all at the same time to the already hyped up crowd. New Jersey was a wonderful melting pot of human and supernatural cultures, and *Serious Moonlight* attracted them all.

Of course. It made perfect sense. Why wouldn't their mother be in the middle of all this? Ariella grinned in her mother's direction.

"I know," she answered George. "I invited her."

Ariella laughed when her brother groaned and held his head as if it was the worst thing in the world to happen. She had three older sisters, and one baby bro, but out of all of them, Ariella was the only one who thought of their mother as her BFF.

Their mom could be quite the handful. Of course, her recent flirtation with the Lion King of their Pride had started several rumors that the two were about to get hitched. But far as Ariella knew, the older, but still hot, Lioness was decidedly ringless.

Good thing, or not? The jury was still out on that one.

Hence, the reason she'd joined her daughter and son for a couple of rounds of tequila shots, and some good old fashioned hell raising, like only those of the Big Cat persuasion could really appreciate. Ari was just depressed enough to want that kind of trouble. After all, things were going nowhere and fast with Brock.

She stood up and looked at her brother with narrowed eyes. It was the kind of look she'd given him as a cub just before she'd pinned his ass to the floor.

"What?" he asked.

Increasing the power of her stare, she almost gave the game away by grinning when he squeaked. Georgie never could best her in that game. Getting the message, he reached for his wallet and dropped two bills on the table.

Having practically licked her plate clean, she purposely left half of George's on the plain white ceramic dish. Brock might be able to ignore her, but if there was one thing that really miffed the big buff doggy, it was when someone didn't finish their food.

Well, tough furballs!

She walked away from the table and left her baby bro to follow, joining their mother with a quick hug and kiss.

"Hey kids! Mama's on a roll," she hooted and pointed to the row of lovely golden shots waiting for them.

The fabulously redheaded Sheila Rand-Crowley smirked as she set a shaker of salt and some sliced limes next to the little shot glasses all lined up like soldiers going off to battle. Ariella supposed they were in a way.

"Hello ladies, and George," Sheila greeted them with a wink.

Ari nodded back. She liked their new princess. A lot. Sheila might be a Dire Wolf Shifter, but she'd married the crowned prince of the Lion Pride and was now officially one of her kin seeing as how Ari was Leo's honorary cousin and all.

"Um, Mom, I don't think—"

"Don't think, Georgie, just have a shot," Patricia Golden said and pressed the small glass against her youngest cub's lips until he had no choice but to swallow the fiery liquid.

Typically, alcohol had little to no effect on Shifters unless—and that was a big UNLESS—it was taken in rapid succession or mixed with one of the handful of herbs whose chemical makeup would render the Shifter's naturally enhanced metabolism nil.

Like *Magibrew*—which was recently banned from this establishment. There were other things that could behave in a similar fashion. Highly concentrated catnip drops could produce the same effect. They were sometimes used to help Lionesses and other feline Shifters during labor, to ease the birthing of one or several cubs. She'd made her mother promise never to trick her into taking that stuff again, so she was not worried.

A mistake, Ariella realized after she swallowed down her first shot, and noted a very familiar and very distinct bitter flavor. Dang it all to heck, it was catnip!

Having been dosed a time or two by her mother and sisters over the years, Ariella knew her stuff. Never George, though. Her baby bro was too much of a stick in the mud for those kinds of shenanigans.

Fucking hell.

The herb was fast-acting when concentrated like this, and her mother would have gotten some very hard to find, medical grade stuff. Her inner Lioness' eyes dilated, and Ariella felt as if her blood was boiling. Confound it, that woman did it again! Her mother had played her.

And here of all the places! She had only minutes before she could become completely uninhibited. And who knew what would happen then? Ariella closed her eyes and turned to confront the woman who'd given birth to her.

"Mom! Did you put catnip in my shot?"

Ariella stomped her foot for affect but her mother waved a manicured hand in her face and made shushing noises.

"Shush up, baby, the band is playing!"

She should have suspected when she'd told her mother the trouble she'd been having with Brock that the woman would resort to some sort of wild extremes to help Ari get his attention.

Prrrr. Good Mama.

Shut up!

She shook her head, trying to ignore her feline and tried to think back to what she'd said to make Patricia lose her dang mind. Ugh. It must have been when she'd confessed to her mother, she suspected Brock was her fated mate. But in her defense, she only expected the woman to just give her some motherly advice or bake cookies or something. She should've known better.

Sigh.

Her mom used to pull stunts like this all the time, but after months of dating King Donovan, Ari thought she'd settled down. Something must've happened between them. Rumors of weddings aside, there must be a reason her mother was acting this way. Ariella's eyes flashed at the woman, who was gyrating like mad in her pleather pants.

My eyes!

"I am not done talkin' to you, Mom. And for

fuck's sake, stop doing that before you bust a seam again!"

"I don't mind givin' them a show, baby girl. If they can't stand the heat, they know what to do!"

Patricia winked and sashayed away, leaving Ariella to follow. A wave of dizziness hit her, and Ari closed her eyes as the effects of the catnip dosed alcohol made themselves known. Not that she was normally a tight ass. Well, not exactly, but Ariella had been working harder than ever lately. Probably had something to do with the fact her mate didn't want her. Just thinking about it made her sad beyond measure, and sad was not how she wanted to feel.

Dance, purred her she-Cat.

The suggestion sounded good to her. She'd often envied normals their ability to have a drink and simply unwind. The problem with her was her pesky supernatural ability to metabolize alcohol. Heck, she'd need a few bottles to even get a buzz.

Catnip laced booze fixed that. Ariella grinned. She had some liquid courage in her now. Heck yeah, she should dance. Sure, her mom's way of bonding with her cubs was unorthodox, but it was fun, and mostly harmless.

Ariella's limbs felt loose as she brought her hands

to her face. She let her cool fingers brush the warm skin of her cheeks and neck, tying back her mane of curly dark hair. She was feeling warmer by the second.

Ari searched the room with half-lidded eyes, head bobbing to the music. Maybe she should embrace this new, uninhibited feeling as a gift from her mother. Yeah. She could do that. Have a little harmless fun, right? After all, she was an unattached female, and she was not getting any younger.

"You feeling alright, Ari?" Sheila interrupted her thoughts.

Ari turned to her cousin-in-law, noting the red eyebrows that seemed to disappear into her hairline as Ariella wobbled a little on her feet.

Oopsies.

CHAPTER 4

The bass was thumping, and the guitar sounded amazing. Serious Moonlight always had the best bands, she thought and shimmied where she stood. Ariella really liked this song. Not usually a dancer, she could hardly keep her hips from moving.

"Ari, did your mother put something in your drink?" Sheila whisper-screamed, leaning over the bar.

"Ow, Sheila my ears! Don't worry about it. My mom is always putting something' in my drink," Ari replied, and giggled.

Wow. She never giggled. Mom must have gotten a higher concentration than she'd had the last time she'd dosed Ari. That was on her spring break eight years ago in Florida.

Ariella had been dumped by her boyfriend the second they'd gotten to their hotel for a skinny Fox Shifter in a two-piece. Miserable and embarrassed, she'd called home and her mom was there within three hours. She'd crashed Ari's vacay, but in a good way.

The week-long festivities had ended with only a couple of tickets and a fine for indecent exposure after she and her mother had been caught lounging naked in the fountain outside of the Miami Grand Hotel.

"Should I call someone for you?" Sheila asked.

"Nah! I'll be *fiiiiiine.*"

Ari nodded her heavy head and stretched her arms wide, spinning in a circle. The only way to get the catnip out of her system was to sweat it out. Simply nothing else to be done, so she might as well enjoy it.

The effects would wear off soon—about twelve hours, judging from last time. And like the last time, hopefully, Ariella's clothes wouldn't be staying on tonight either. Staying a virgin was just not appealing at the moment.

"I got it!" Ari said aloud with a wicked grin plastered on her face.

"You got what, honey?" Sheila asked.

"The solution to all my problems!"

"Oh, fuck" the she-Wolf grumbled.

But Ari was not going to let her bring her down. She knew what she had to do to get out of this rut she seemed stuck in. Ari was going to lose her virginity to some lucky guy, and afterward, she would use her newly acquired seductive wiles and smexy time skills to find a mate despite Brock Laurent!

"Ariella, please tell me what is going on in that head of yours," Sheila said, taking hold of Ari's hand.

"I got it all figured out, cuz. No more rejected mate blues for me. I know what I'm gonna do," Ariella told her.

She squeezed the woman's hand and smiled like the cat who ate the canary. Her plan was a little foggy, but Ari blamed that on her catnip and tequila soaked brain. It would all come together. It had to.

Her mother, who upon closer observation turned out to be wearing a pair of practically painted-on leopard-spotted pleather pants—a sort of irony if you will, being everyone knew Lionesses were better than Leopards any day—was currently shaking and grinding between two enormously buff strangers.

"Mom!" she yelled, but Patricia waved her away.

For an older woman, Patricia Golden sure knew how to get her groove on. She was her hero and Ariella knew she was lucky to have Patty as a mom. The older feline would know just how to help Ariella lose her maidenhead.

Then maybe she could forget all about men who didn't want their mates.

"Earth to Ariella. Hey, talk to me, honey. What are you talking about?"

Sheila seemed to be speaking rather slowly, but Ari just winked at her. Silly she-Wolf. So lucky to have her mate. She just did not understand Ariella's predicament. Grabbing the bottle of tequila from the bar, Ari chugged the last of it.

"You are sweet to worry about me, Sheila, but I got a plan. I'm gonna lose my virginity tonight," she said.

"What did you say?" Sheila shook her head and pointed to her ears.

Dang it. Her friend couldn't hear her above the noise.

"I said," Ariella yelled loudly—*and wouldn't you*

know it, the band stopped playing that exact moment. "I'm going to lose my virginity tonight!"

She looked around and laughed loudly as the rowdy group of bar goers applauded and cheered her on. Giggling at their encouragement, she took off to join her mother on the dance floor.

"You go, girl!"

"I can help with that."

"Virginity is overrated!"

"I'd tap that!"

"Hey, knock it off!" Sheila yelled at the customers still waiting for their drinks.

"I can fix your problem, baby," one of the strangers said, and Ariella giggled.

He wasn't even unpleasant looking. Maybe finding a sex partner wouldn't be as difficult as she thought.

"Back off, buddy, or you are out of here! Shit. Ariella, don't you move," Sheila ordered and grabbed her cell phone from behind the bar, but Ari was already walking away.

She felt too good and loose for any yelling and nonsense. Ari didn't want to do anything but have a good time. What was so wrong with that?

The music was loud and sounded like a carnival

ride. Between the band and the lights, and the catnip of course, Ariella felt young and pretty and alive for the first time in a long while. The crowd was bouncing up and down joyously and she joined them, clapping her hands and shaking her booty for all she was worth.

"Hey, baby girl. You look great," her mother yelled.

"Thanks, Mom. I feel pretty great," she yelled back.

"That's good, honey. I got that *'nip* from a new guy. It's supposed to be extra potent," her mother informed her with a winked.

"Mama, I think I want to lose my virginity tonight," Ariella yelled into her mother's ear while keeping up with the bopping and swaying.

"Okay, honey, but be careful," her mother said.

Patricia Golden pinched her daughter's cheek, then turned around to dance with a very tall and thin older man with an Aussie accent. One sniff and Ari was sure he had to be an Ostrich Shifter. Again, thoughts of their Pride leader plagued her, but that was her mom's affair, not hers. She'd learned early to stay out of her mother's love life.

Ariella hated to admit it, but this was the best she

had felt in weeks. Not something she expected after meeting her fated mate. But then again, nothing had gone as planned since she laid eyes on Brock Laurent. All her childhood fantasies of happy-ever-after's had been tossed to the wind the second he walked away from her.

Bastard never even looked back.

That was it. She was done. She'd tried everything she knew to get him to acknowledge what they were to each other, short of tattooing the words *claim me already* on her forehead—or as her brother George insisted, Ariella was rocking a solid a fivehead—five fingers fit on her forehead. Gods, she hated her brother sometimes.

Jerk.

Sniff.

Whatever. If her forehead was big, it was because she was a smarty pants. That's what Mom always said in her defense. Anyway, back to that dang dog boy. NO matter what she did, Brock still stubbornly refused to accept she was made for him. It was both insulting and infuriating.

What was so bad about her, anyway? What was so horrible that he didn't want her?

Ariella wasn't ugly. Heck, she was downright cute, even if she wasn't blonde, regardless of what her snooty cousins said. She'd spent the last few months alternating between lust and anger for the hunky Dire Wolf. But no more. She decided tonight was her night and it was time to check out her options.

Like the big, *sniff* , Bison Shifter, who'd sided up to her during the band's lively cover of *Paradise City*. Ariella always was a *Guns N' Roses* fan. If she squinted hard, the stranger kinda looked like Slash.

They jumped and swayed, clapped, and sang along until the stranger felt secure enough to lean down and whisper in her ear. He smelled a little like hay, but that was alright, she supposed.

"Hey, baby, how about we get out of here?" he grunted against her ear, and his beard kind of tickled her skin.

"Well, I was planning on losing my virginity tonight. I'm interviewing for the position, you interested?"

"Hell yeah. I can help with that, baby," he returned, and she smiled at him through a haze of tequila and catnip.

His hair was curlier than hers, she thought giddily and nodded her head. Sounded like a plan. She could finally have sex, just to see what the fuss was about, then she could walk away.

Isn't that what men did? No strings sex?

Yep, that was a damn fine idea. She looked at the big man and frowned. He seemed even bigger than before.

"Hey," she said, swaying slightly. "Are you getting taller or am I shrinking?"

"Aghhh!" the Bison Shifter yelped.

Before Ariella could utter a response, she noticed a pair of big hands gripping the Bison by his wide shoulders. Suddenly, the man was flying through the air.

"Hey! We didn't even get busy yet?" she growled, disappointed.

Next thing she knew, Ari was staring into the steely blue eyes of the one man she'd just given up on. Her heart pounded, and she felt both bitterly disappointed and confused when she looked at the outrageously handsome Dire Wolf.

"Ariella," he growled her name, and she seemed to sober up for a split second as every inch of her went on high alert—*like it always did around him.*

Brock was the only man in the whole world who could make her Lioness purr like a kitten. Damn him.

"Geez, Brock," she shouted and stomped her booted feet. "I was gonna have sex with him!"

"The hell you were," he growled, and she wanted to roar her outrage.

Stupid pussy-blocking, butt-sniffing, asshat!

"Ooh, you make me so mad," she stomped her foot one more time and narrowed her eyes at the snooty Wolf.

"Ariella, I am warning you—"

"Oh, are *you* warning *me*? You know what? You can just *eat my fur*!"

Even as she yelled the old childhood taunt, the same one she and her siblings used to taunt each other, her inner, perverted she-Cat had another type of eating in mind instantaneously.

Traitor, she scolded her feline, but it was no good.

Brock crowded her personal space, and before she knew it, his face was directly in front of hers. She breathed in his forest fresh scent, and damn if she didn't feel even more intoxicated from that one good whiff of him.

"Why do you always smell so good?" she asked, but did he answer?

Of course not. Ariella huffed out a breath and turned to walk away when he stopped her with a hand on her arm.

"Mine," Brock growled so softly she almost missed it.

Ariella blinked up at him in sheer surprise at the possessive one-syllable word. Next, he scooped her up in his big, strong arms and walked out of the bar with her. Where he was going, she didn't know, but oh, could she hope.

Yes, please. Prrrrrr.

CHAPTER 5

"*I was gonna have sex with him—*"

That damn sentence was on repeat inside his head. Anger, rage, and a certain green-eyed monster sat on his shoulder, egging him on as Brock carried the squirming female outside, through the woods, and to the small stream that ran across the property in back of the Dire Wolf Pack house.

Ever since he'd met the woman, he hadn't been able to think straight. Right then, he could hardly see two feet in front of him. His Wolf was snarling and snapping at the image of that fucking asshole. Fucking Bison Shifter. He obviously wanted to go home missing a hoof or two for touching his Ariella.

My Ariella? No. She's not mine.

Yes, she is, his beast argued.

Fuck. Brock was shaking with emotion. No, he hadn't claimed her, but that didn't make his Wolf any less possessive about the little wildcat.

Okay, fine. He was an asshole. He'd freely admit it, but there was a reason he hadn't rushed into things with the woman. But yeah, he was a prick for keeping that reason to himself.

Maybe it was time they had a serious discussion. Of course, not now. Not when she was three sheets to the wind and probably wouldn't remember half of what they said. Brock would have laughed if there was any chance she wouldn't get even more pissed off at him.

As it was, the normally sweet and shy Ariella was busy punching, kicking, and cursing him out. She wasn't hurting him, but damn, the woman had some wiggle to her. Brock was trying his damndest not to drop her on her fine ass.

Grrrrr.

He hadn't needed Sheila's text to tell him there was trouble. Between Phoenix and his own senses, he'd anticipated it before it happened. Of course, he did not know she would proclaim her virginity so spectacularly.

Saturday night and the place had been crowded as all get out when she'd made her announcement.

His head snapped to the side, and he thought he heard something in the woods. This part of their property was private, but that didn't mean the odd patron didn't try sneaking around back there despite their security measures.

A virgin. Fuck.

He'd known it, but that wasn't the same as having her shout it. It seemed tattooed inside his brain. Maybe not tattooed. Maybe more like a neon sign flashing on and off with the word virgin in bold letters.

Ariella was a virgin.

Mine. Claim. Now.

Fucking hell.

A part of him felt even more ferociously possessive of her now. Unfortunately, so did half the fucking bar. If there was one thing Shifter males coveted, it was claiming a virgin bride. Don't ask why. Fucking Neanderthals, the lot of them. Apparently, he was no different. Once he'd thought those words, they got stuck in his brain.

Virgin bride. My virgin mate.

A picture of Ariella decked out in a white gown made of silk and lace flashed through his mind and his Wolf growled appreciatively. She'd be a beautiful bride. His beautiful bride.

No.

Grrr.

"Stop squirming or we are both gonna wind up on the ground," he chided as he stepped over a mound of fallen leaves.

"Brock! You put me down right now," she yelled and wiggled, but he only held her tighter.

Having his arms full of the voluptuous, sweet smelling, tempting as hell she-Cat might have been hell on his nerves, but damn, it was sweet to hold her. It was all he could do not to turn his head and give her a love bite on her plump cheek.

Her musky scent invaded his nostrils, and Brock was drowning in it. He would give anything to taste her. To memorize every nuance of her unique flavor. Putting one foot in front of the other was a chore. She made him lose all focus and reason.

Finally, he got them to the grassy shore of the creek. Brock hoisted her princess style into his arms, and Ariella's large amber eyes appeared confused. She yelped and clutched at his shoulders.

"You'll drop me," she hissed, and he raised one eyebrow and growled his reply.

Silly she-Cat, he could more than handle her weight. The thing that was driving him crazy was her scent, and the fact her chest was heaving. Even through the loose sweater she wore, he could make out the swell of what he knew were perfect breasts.

Sexy sexy woman.

She was full and round as a woman should be. More than enough to make his mouth water. It might be poor timing, but fuck it. Brock dropped a hard kiss on her open mouth and watched her eyes flash with heat just before they opened wide as she realized his intentions.

"Hold your nose, kitten," he growled and tossed her into the icy water before she could reply.

Little hellcat needed to sober up before he told her what he had in mind for the two of them. Of course, he had no idea if a dunk in the creek could freeze the catnip out of her. He was going to have to chat with her mother, and soon. Having been told of the older Lioness' hijinks by both Phoenix and Sheila, the latter of whom had called him minutes ago with the news that his would-be-mate had just announced her intention to lose her virginity to the entire bar. Thank fuck Brock had already been on his way inside.

He'd almost swallowed his tongue when he'd heard that little blip of information. That she was pristine and untouched in this day and age somehow resonated with his primordial beast.

Caveman much?

Fuck yes.

His Dire Wolf was prehistoric in more ways than one. He wouldn't apologize for it. Brock never claimed to be anything other than what he was. Imperfect and wholly unrepentant. It was just another reason for his whole *hands off* approach to Ariella.

He'd seen the half-eaten plate of food she'd left on her table. The waitress had almost peed herself at having to tell him what she said. Little minx. Brock wasn't conceited, but he knew there were two things in life he did very well. One was ride. The other was cook. If Ariella didn't finish a meal he'd prepared, it was a message. One he would ponder another time. He was currently busy making sure she was staying afloat in the creek.

"You sober yet?" he asked.

"Dammit!" she sputtered and struggled to keep her head above the surface.

Ariella could typically swim like a fish—*yes, he knew that from spying on her.* But she was having a hard time now. He frowned. She must've been more affected by the catnip than he'd previously thought.

"Ariella, you, okay?" he asked as she spit out some of the water she'd swallowed back into the stream.

"No! I'm freezing and I'm all tangled in my skirt. Brock, get me out of here," she wailed.

"You can do it. Come on, swim to the side. Well, put a little effort into it," he chided, uncertain whether the little minx was angling for a way to splash him.

"My clothes are dragging me down," she gasped and went back under.

Hell, he should've considered that seeing as how it was early Spring and she'd been wearing a long flowy skirt with leather boots and a creamy white sweater that left one shoulder deliciously bare.

Fine. Yes, he paid attention to her. Any detail he could take in, study, agonize over late at night. His Wolf was snarling at him to hurry up and dive in, but he hesitated. She was a Shifter and should have had no problem staying afloat.

"Stop playing around, Ariella," he frowned and waited a beat.

Shit.

This wasn't good. When she didn't come immediately back up, Brock panicked. His Wolf snarled and snapped, and he cursed soundly before jumping in clothes and all.

"Ari?" he yelled and dove beneath the chilly

water, searching for her among the tall grass and rocks.

It was dark and murky, and he couldn't see shit, never mind the fact his sense of smell did not work in water. His Wolf was agitated, furious at him, and he was more than happy to let the beast chew him out, but not yet. Not till after he found her. He breached the surface to suck in more air before preparing to dive back under.

Of course, he should've known better than to panic. The sassy little minx was waiting for him behind one of the larger boulders that sat at the bottom of the creek. She must have great lungs, he mused after Ariella snagged his foot and pulled him down.

"Yip," he squeaked—*to his Wolf's unending shame,* Going under and swallowing a mouthful of creek water.

She was a Lioness, so he should have known she was strong. But damn, Ariella was really *really* strong. More than he'd imagined she would be. She held him under easily, causing his chest to burn, but in a good way.

The game was officially on.

They wrestled under the water playfully. She got him good a few times, but Brock soon got the advantage and made it to the surface with her in tow. He sucked in the cool, fresh air greedily, watching Ariella's pretty pink-cheeked face as she did the same.

"Have you had enough?" he asked.

"Not on your life," she growled, just before tackling him once more.

Brock barked out a laugh as he caught the wily and surprisingly sporty woman. He was stunned at the vigorous rough play and the fact that she was so at ease with him after months of her shyly watching him with those killer amber eyes and deliciously pouty mouth.

Ariella was using her Shifter's natural agility and strength against him. Shocked and full of admiration, he damn near had his ass handed to him in this unexpected bout of underwater wrestling. He could hardly believe it.

What Shifter male could resist a bit of frolicking with a sexy female? This luscious little tidbit had been haunting his dreams ever since he'd met her.

"I thought you were afraid of me," he growled when she landed on his back and tried to pull him under.

"Afraid of a big ol' puppy dog? Never! I eat dogs for breakfast," she snarled and snapped her impressive teeth.

So, she thought she could get the best of him, did she? After vying for dominance, he finally over-whelmed her with a tickle pinch combination that had her yowling and calling mercy.

"You give?" he asked, wrapping his arms around her waist, and pulling her tempting body as close as he dared.

She was so small compared to him. Positively tiny. Fragile even.

Brock worried for a moment that he'd been too rough, but there she was, smiling up at him like a naughty little siren. He never would have guessed she would hide in the cool water, dragging him under for some aquatic rough housing.

He was surprised and, for the first time in a while, Brock had fun. It had been a long time since he could say that for real. She looked beautiful with her hair all wet, floating around her shoulders.

Of course, if he could ignore the throbbing boner in his soaked chef's pants, that was all this would be —*harmless fun.*

But it was more than that. Everything about her was enticing from the rivulets of water that rolled down her cheek, to her neck, and down her chest to disappear somewhere in her generous cleavage.

Damn, that drop of water had the life!

He wanted to follow its path with his mouth and tongue. Brock wanted her. The strength of his desire gave him pause, but she didn't seem to mind it. Not even when she brushed up against that part of him, he was certain would terrify the sweet little innocent.

Surely, if she was afraid of someone his size, she would've jumped or distanced herself, but not Ariella. She kept her hands on his shoulders and her body close to his even as he treaded water with her in his arms. Thank goodness they were in the shallower end of the stream.

"Okay, I give," she said and laughed. "But just for a minute. I need to catch my breath."

Her eyes sparkled with mischief, and she laid her head down on Brock's shoulder, allowing him to hug her even closer. The contact was shocking, as it was novel. Her body was warm despite the water. This was as close as he'd ever been to Ariella except for when she'd ridden on his Harley. They played under the cold water until his lungs felt like they were going to burst, and he frowned. She must be tired. That and the catnip were why she snuggled closer.

Tell yourself that, his Wolf grunted.

Fuck.

She was going to be the death of him. He exhaled

slowly, and Ariella simply sighed in contentment. During their games, she had flung off her sweater and had been tormenting him with hints of her lacy bra and pale skin as she played in and out of the water. She sat up, and he accommodated her with both his hands cupping her sweet ass. Ariella wrapped her legs around his waist, and her lace-covered breasts were pressed against his unfortunately still-covered chest.

"I got you good, didn't I?" she said breathlessly, laughing as her dark hair clung to her scalp.

Her cheeks were pink from either the cold or the exertion. Or maybe from the effects of the catnip and booze. Either way, between that and the way her mascara was slightly smudged, making her thick lashes stick together, the feline looked positively adorable.

Pretty pussy cat. Tempting. Perfect. Ours.

In truth, he had never seen a woman look more beautiful. He felt his Wolf peek through his eyes and knew what the animal wanted, but Brock forced the beast down. He had to resist her, even though she was clinging sweetly to his shoulders so closely that her warm breath tickled his earlobe.

"I haven't had this much fun since the fourth of

July when Mom put magicked sparklers in everyone's drinks at the Pride's annual barbecue."

"What happened?" he asked, curious about her, wanting to know more.

Fuck, he was pathetic. Brock should know better. He should stay away. But he was greedy for any snippet of information he could glean about her life.

"Well, Mama has always been a joker. So, at one o'clock in the morning, every single sparkler she'd given out went off—and with a bang, at that! There were tiny fires everywhere. Half the Lion Shifters who came to the event, especially the ones who were stupid enough to wear too much hairspray, went home soaking wet after their fires had been put out, with hats and scarves wrapped around their heads, and scowls on their faces. My cousin Layla's beauty salon was booked solid for a month, and she had to special order hair extensions from overseas after buying out every supply store in the states," Ariella told him, laughing out loud the entire time she told the story.

The sound of her joy was intoxicating, contagious even. But it was more than that. Her voice, her enthusiasm, and her general openness were just plain refreshing. Like a pinch of bright lemon zest, the kind he sometimes added to brighten up recipes.

That was his Ariella to a T. She was his own personal *pinch of sass.* Changing his point of view, shaking things up, and making him stop and smell the roses.

How many years had he spent alone? Always riding on the open road with his Pack with no end in sight. How many lonely miles sat between him and a conversation such as this one?

Fuck. Be honest, his Wolf snapped.

He'd never had a conversation like this one. She blinked up at him, mouth slightly open in a half smile as she waited for some reaction from him. That was his cue and, to his surprise, he found himself wanting to talk with her.

"Interesting party," he answered and almost moaned aloud when her spicy, musky scent filled his nostrils and his lungs.

She smelled divine and if he was a wagering Wolf, he'd bet on her tasting even better. As a chef, Brock knew when he was choosing ingredients which were best by scent alone, and Ariella was the best of everything he'd ever come across.

There was nothing false or overly sweet about her. No cloying perfume or globs of face paint hiding her from him. Ariella was natural and unblemished, superb in her raw beauty, and he wanted more of it. More of her. Like the finest spices and top shelf herbs, she was rare and unique.

Mine.

He'd been fighting a losing battle. Insects chirping, the sounds of flowing water, and the steady night breeze made a symphony around them, but all he could hear was his and Ariella's hearts beating in time. His Dire Wolf pushed him for more, but he held steady.

Once upon a time, young Brock had thought himself in love and the rejection was still sharp in his mind. But was he doomed to live in the past forever? Brock shook his head, and grabbing his nerve, he leaned down and brushed her lips with his.

He might be unsure of Ariella's reaction to him in bed, to the reception he would get from a virgin, but he was downright cocky about his ability to kiss her mindless. So he did.

Ariella moaned gently and opened for his invasion while he kicked his feet to keep them afloat.

"Oh, Brock," she moaned as his lips traveled from her mouth to her cheek and her neck.

"Ariella," he ground out against her skin and held her tighter.

This was it. His big moment.

Brock was going to tell her, to confront her—no,

to confess to her that *yes*, he was aware of what they were to each other. A knot formed in his stomach, and his heart threatened to beat him to death. He had to tell her why he'd been denying them and delaying the inevitable.

Do it now.

"Ariella, I need to talk to you," he began and tried to fight the gnawing fear that had built up to incredible proportions suddenly. "Ari?"

Turned out Brock had zero reason to worry. Expelling a deep, calming breath, he narrowed his eyes as his burden grew unexpectedly limp in the cool water.

Since when was his hellcat a plaint, submissive female? One look down told him all he needed to know about her unusual complacency.

His golden goddess, his little hellcat, his sweet, lovely, and virginal Ariella had passed out on him.

Grrrrrrrr.

CHAPTER 6

"I never want to drink again!" Patricia Golden groaned and held on to the wall as she stumbled forward.

Her short velvet robe and oversized bunny slippers were horrifying, but Ariella was grateful for them. Last time her mother had crashed her apartment, she had walked around the next day in the nude on account of losing her clothes somewhere between the bar and home.

Yikes.

She was still having nightmares. She shivered at the memory and watched her mother slink all the way to the coffeepot. It was her favorite appliance in the world. The stainless steel goddess inspired machine sat on the counter and filled the kitchen with the strong fragrance of freshly brewed, aromatic, revitalizing, lifesaving coffee.

"This is the nectar of the gods, baby girl!"

"Shhhh!"

Ariella hushed her mom. Her head was still buzzing like she had a hive of bees floating inside. She would never forgive the woman for this. Crazy she-Cat had dosed Ariella—her youngest baby daughter—with a high potency herbal supplement meant for she-Cats in labor, for fuck's sake. And at *Serious Moonlight* of all places.

Prrrrrrrrr.

Her kitty was still acting as if the night had been some kind of success, but she did not know why. The level of embarrassment Ariella felt was something she didn't think she'd ever get over. And now she had to rush into work for an emergency meeting.

Crap. Crap. CRAP.

She growled and grabbed her cell. The stupid thing had been going off all weekend. Ariella looked down and opened the text from anonymous and found a giant dancing eggplant gif.

Perfect. Just perfect.

"Not another one!"

"Shhhh, baby girl, please. I carried you for nine

months, and I think the least you can do is give me some quiet," her mother moaned.

"This is your fault, Mom. When are you going to stop, already?"

"Stop what? I was only trying to get you to loosen up, baby girl."

"Ugh. Well, I got loose alright," she mumbled, unable to stay angry with her mother for any real amount of time.

Besides, worse things had happened after going on one of her mother's adventures. So, what if Ariella announced her virginity to the entire bar? Big deal, right?

Well, she'd been getting spam calls and PMs on all her social media accounts from dozens of men, and a few women, ever since. Even operating at less than a hundred percent, she'd managed to identify a few fake accounts belonging to her sisters and her awful cousins, offering lewd suggestions.

Those perverse pussies. Ugh.

They were always big on the texts, but never to her face. Still, she admitted as she sipped her coffee and scrolled through her messages, there were some halfway decent *indecent proposals* in there.

Many of whom were offering to relive her of her little problem in the most imaginative of ways. What exactly was an Eiffel tower? And did she need to not shave her armpits to do it?

Hmmm.

"Oh, gawd! Eat my fur," she muttered and blocked another pervert, who'd stupidly sent her a video of his limp and unimpressive member.

Like that was gonna seal the deal, pal! Whatevah.

Ariella rolled her eyes. She might be green as spring grass when it came to actually having sex, but she knew it took a little more than a Tootsie Roll, for Pete's sake!

"Oh, even my eyes hurt," Patricia moaned into her steaming mug of coffee.

Of course, she'd used the one shaped like an enormous purple wang, drinking from the tip deeply. Her mother had the most obscene tastes, but Ariella adored the woman.

"Serves you right," she mumbled and glared at her mother. "What is going on with you, Mom? Are you moving back in? Did something happen with you and King Donovan?"

"I am not discussing that right now, child. Hey, it's a full moon this week. Did you know that? Oh, look at the time! Get going. You have work, right?"

"I'm going, I'm going, sheesh," Ariella mumbled, shaking her head.

That woman could have a full discussion and never let another person make a sound! She grabbed her purse, slipping on her lowest pair of heels before taking off for another fun filled workday.

Snark snark snark.

The cutesy little smart car was adorable when driving in her little hometown of Blue Valley, but she would never take it on the highway. The tiny lime green two-seater would be little more than a coffin if it came up against an eighteen-wheeler. She only used it to go to and from work and the condo she sometimes shared with her mother.

Patricia had been spending so much time at the palace lately, Ari wondered if she'd be living alone soon. She secretly believed the rumors that the now hearty and healthy King had fallen for her mom, but maybe, like some men she knew but would not name, Donovan Crowley just couldn't come around to actually making a commitment.

Poor Mom.

Ariella frowned thoughtfully as she pulled into a free parking space outside her office. The *Eat Well Live Proud* building was not as big as some international corporations, but it suited the Pride just fine.

Keeping the supernatural world secret was tantamount to every organization run by Shifters regardless of personal agenda. The Pride had done well, developing the land bought and paid for by the royal family into a gated community complete with business section. It was like the Lions had their own little world, and Ariella grew up pampered and protected compared to some.

Nerves filled her stomach as she thought about her workday. Competition was fierce and she was still feeling hungover from the catnip, and other things. She could have sworn she'd been skinny dipping with Brock, but that couldn't be right. Could it?

Gulp. Game face, girl.

She could not let her guard down here. Maybe later she would shift to her Lioness and go for a quick run. There was a gorgeous patch of forest running parallel to the Pride lands. Some of it was owned by them, some owned by the Dire Wolves on the other side of the creek she'd bathed in last night.

Shit. There went her mind again, traveling forbidden paths. She could not afford to slip up today, or everything she'd been working for the past six months would have been for nothing.

Back to her thoughts of romping through woods. Yes, they did lead to private property owned by the

DWMC. But it was easy to avoid their land. If that was what she wanted to do. Of course, Ari's beast knew a shortcut through the trees that led to the parking lot behind *Serious Moonlight* and the Dire Wolf Pack House. Not that she ever took that route. Well, not lately, anyway.

Or had she?

Just how did Ari make it home last night? She recalled waking up at five o'clock in the morning, glaring at the neon green numbers on her old-fashioned alarm clock. She had several of the things around the house, otherwise she might never wake up. Cats loved to sleep. Even Shifter Cats.

Hmmm.

She grabbed her bag, exiting the vehicle and tried to recall her steps last night. She could have sworn she had been swimming, and yet, Ariella had woken up in dry clothes in her own bed. Last thing she remembered was dancing and getting propositioned by a stranger. Her attempt at flirting back had been cut short by Brock.

Actually, the angry Dire Wolf had tossed her would-be-deflowerer, aka the Slash lookalike, across the bar. He then picked her up, curvy ass and all, and carried her out of the bar.

Shivers racked her body at the remembered

touches, and Ariella didn't know whether to laugh or cry. He had seen her at her absolute worst. True, it was the longest she'd ever spent alone in his company. And even if, from what she recalled, it had been thrilling for her, Brock would probably avoid her more than ever now.

She'd been thoroughly under the influence of catnip infused tequila, but Ari still had a wonderful time. OMG! Had Brock really kissed her? She racked her brain for proof or some sign she was making that part up—call it wishful thinking, but no, even her she-Cat seemed certain.

Okay. So they kissed. Ohmyfuckinggawd!

Her heart was pounding her to death as she worried about what had happened. Kissing Brock was like the culmination of all her daydreams over the past few months. Ariella had had boyfriends, but she never really liked kissing them. What if she sucked at it?

Crap.

That was it. She totally sucked at it. After all, she had woken up alone. If she'd been good at kissing, she highly doubted a healthy male would have left it at that. How much more embarrassing were her memories going to get? Ugh. Ari tripped over a crooked slap of the sidewalk as the dreaded thought entered her brain.

Okay, she needed to remain calm. Ari had kissed boys before. They just never seemed able to handle her exuberance. Sure, boys had wanted to have sex with her, just no one she was interested in that way. After all, Ari couldn't give herself to someone who needed to take frequent breaks from just making out.

But that was what she typically attracted—skinny mama's boys with no idea how to handle her. She needed an apex predator. A strong one. None of the males in her Pride were interested in any of the Golden sisters.

Especially not after Adrianna had damn near castrated her high school boyfriend for cheating on her. It had been slim pickings from then on for all four of them, truth be told. Speak of the devil, Ariella damn near jumped out of her skin when her sister grabbed her arm.

"Ari, you coming inside or what?" Adrianna asked.

"Eeek! Holy fuck, Adrianna! Make some damn noise next time you sneak up on a bitch," she growled.

"Ha! I heard someone got in the catnip last night," she replied in an annoying sing-song voice.

Ariella just grunted. Annabeth and Antonette were waiting inside, and she cringed at the thought of what her three siblings had in store for her. Pranksters, all of them. Best to just get it over with.

Ari heaved a sigh and readjusted her purse on her shoulder. The great kissing question would just have to wait. Newly mated Annabeth was trying unsuccessfully to hide a smirk as Ari walked by. That she-Cat never could hold in a giggle.

Brats. All of them. They were definitely pulling something Ari. As the baby of the four, Ariella was used to it. Generally, she was a good sport about things like that, but her nerves were positively frayed at the moment. She only hoped they didn't go overboard.

The Golden sisters were not typically meanspirited. But shit had been known to go too far sometimes. Like when Ad put hair removal cream in Toni's leave-in conditioner before prom senior year. That one was particularly memorable since the cat fight that broke out between them had destroyed their grandmother's last remaining tea set. Good thing Nana hadn't cared a fig for tea. She'd been too busy shouting instructions at her fighting grand-daughters.

Ariella supposed it was her turn to take some heat. After all, they had all ganged up on Annabeth when she'd come home with a mate a few months back. Of course, the sexified gift basket they left was bird themed for her new Falcon Shifter mate. If you asked Ariella, it was downright thoughtful of them. Especially, the sun butter part. That had been her idea.

The time before that, Toni had been in the hot seat. It was her own fault though. She was the one who woke up stark naked on the Palace lawn with Gavin Green, a Rabbit Shifter from town, with a half-eaten bowl of banana pudding and one green flip-flop between them. Adrianna and Ariella took photos—how could they not?

They even sent the images to a couple of producers of pornographic magazines and Toni had received no less than twelve offers. Rumor had it she was to be featured in the *Naughty or Nice Christmas Charity Calendar* which was rumored to be Shifter run non-profit that selected a different cause every year as beneficiary.

Ariella couldn't blame her if she posed for them.

Toni was simply gorgeous and had a rockin' bod. Besides, it was for charity.

"So, how are you?" Annabeth asked, interrupting her musings.

"Fine."

Ariella squinted. She was sure Annabeth would crack, but the brat turned her head with a squeak. Being mated must have given her some backbone. Lucky beyotch.

"I see," Adrianna said, coming between the two of them. "Nothing you'd like to discuss, honey?"

"Like what?"

"Well, if you ever need advice on, *you know,* anything," Toni said, tucking one hand in the crook of Ari's elbow and waving the other one in the air.

"What is wrong with you three?" Ariella asked. She did not trust them at all. Not one little bitty bit.

"Nothing!"

"Sheesh."

"Can't sisters just be nice?"

"Wait a second. It can't be true! Didn't you bang *Hairy Henry* on prom weekend?" Annabeth asked in a stage whisper.

"*Oh my gawd!* Shut up, Annabeth. And no, I didn't bang *Hairy Henry,*" she whisper screamed back at her nosy sibling, painfully aware of the questioning eyes of her coworkers and Pride mates surrounding them.

What the heck was going on? Fucking hell. This was going to be awful. She just knew it. Practically felt it in her gut.

"Well, I mean, Mom said you found your mate, so we were just shocked when the tweets went out about you still being a virgin and all," Annabeth said and shrugged.

"Tweets? I saw it in a TikTok," Adrianna added.

Ariella groaned.

"Oh no. Please tell me she didn't," she moaned, covering her face with her eyes.

"Wish we could, cupcake," Adrianna added.

"Mommy dearest sent out a Pride wide alert asking for help in *devirginizing* her youngest daughter," Annabeth informed her.

"I will put hair remover in every single bottle of shampoo in all of your apartments, I swear on my firstborn," Ariella growled, and tried to stop the tide of embarrassment that was currently threatening to drown her.

"Well, we're in luck then, sister. Cause if you ain't getting' any, you ain't havin' any cubs," Toni snarked, a wicked grin splitting her pretty face.

Beyotches. All of them.

Ariella could not believe it. Her own mother had outed her. Again. That was it. She was so going to show everyone the pictures of her mother, *pre-bikini wax*, she'd been holding over the female's head.

"Alright, I get Mom's lunacy, but you three are behaving very suspiciously. What did you do?"

Ariella quirked an eyebrow and followed them down the hall, noting the snickers and giggles from her co-workers as she walked to her desk.

"Now, don't get mad," Adrianna began seriously, but ruined it by snorting.

That was when Ariella saw it. The mother of all pranks. Right on her desk inside the offices of *Eat Well Live Proud*, her place of business, where she had a reputation to uphold, was an enormous gift basket.

"You had it coming," Annabeth said in a singsong voice, and she was not wrong.

After all, Ari had gleefully taken part in a similar such thing for Annabeth. Only, this was her place of work, and this basket was not fruit and stale crackers with awful nuts and cheese that no one liked.

Nope. This was filled with other things. Scandalous, gossip producing, funny if it was happening to someone else, horrifyingly embarrassing things.

Sigh.

Her coworkers, which included three sisters, eighteen cousins, and various other Pride members, stood around smirking and giggling as Ariella's eyes grew wide with horror. Naturally, the most prominent object inside the oversized basket that was topped for some reason with a big pink glitter ribbon was a stuffed poodle.

The dayglo purple pooch was about four feet high and sporting a strap-on which happened to have the biggest, pink glow-in-the-dark dildo Ariella had ever seen. Not to mention the pink leather ball-gag tied around the pornographic puppy's neck.

Next to the dildo dog was an assortment of vibrators, nipple clamps, whips, chains, and—*oh shit* —a straight up gallon of strawberry flavored lube. There was also a thick, hardcover copy of a fully illustrated Kama Sutra, translated by a Harvard scholar, apparently. Beside it were more instructional books on *how to train your puppy*.

Dog collars, leashes, a box of *wee wee* pads, and an assortment of rawhide and chew toys were scattered throughout. Not to mention, a giant box of peanut butter flavored dog treats, and a giant jar of peanut butter. The creamy kind.

"We just thought we could help you snag that dog

you're after," announced Adrianna to a round of laughter and applause.

"What the hell is going on here?" her boss, Maggie Pierce, one of the King's new circle, yelled from the doorway and everyone snapped to attention.

"Um, nothing," Ariella answered.

She clapped a hand over her mouth, trying to stand in front of the giant dildo basket, but to no avail. Her boss did not like smarty pants. Especially anyone who was dumb enough to answer what was clearly a rhetorical question.

Shit.

This was not good.

"Well, if you are all finished with what I am going to assume is a basket of dog training supplies, maybe we can get on with the meeting and our workday. Oh, and Ariella, while I appreciate your virtue is the gossip of the hour, let's keep it down until after work, shall we?" Ms. Pierce snarled.

"Yes, ma'am," she replied in a low voice.

"Good. Get that basket out of here. Now."

"Yes, ma'am," Ariella whispered again.

She lugged the tremendous thing down to her tiny car where it took up all of her trunk, even spilling over to the passenger seat, which she had to lay down. Ariella bit her lip and wondered if the strap-on was visible from the outside now that she had a ball gag wearing purple poodle as a passenger.

FML.

She groaned and ran back inside. Ariella was only fifteen minutes late to the meeting. Mrs. Pierce waited until the end of her long drawn out speech over new import laws and procedures at the docks to announce the top contenders for this quarter's leaders.

Ariella held her breath when the top three were announced. The entire room did, as a matter of fact. Call it a predator's need to win, whatever it was, this quarterly contest was very motivational.

Ariella had never won. Not once. She'd been very determined this time around. Had worked her butt off too. What else did she have going for her at the moment?

Besides Fluffy, her new BFF that was waiting in her car. Sigh.

"Well, ladies and gents, this has never happened before, but it seems there is a tie for the lead between Cornelia Higgins and Ariella Golden," Ms. Pierce announced,

"You have a few more days till we close out the contest. Good luck, you two."

"Ari, that's great!" Adrianna whispered.

Her sisters accompanied her, while her work friends offered congratulations, as she walked back out to her desk. She was both happy and bummed. Ari just couldn't believe after all her hard work, she was still tied with Cornelia Higgins. How did that woman do it?

Well, it was her own fault for pussyfooting around the *Serious Moonlight* account, and not going in for the kill. She'd already hit up every other small business in the area.

She needed that Wolf run bar, and not just half of what she offered. Ari needed to get *all* their business, darn it. Freaking Brock was standing in her way. The only reason he'd ever offered even a portion of their business to Ariella was because of her connection to Leo, Sheila's mate.

Rawrrr.

Her Lioness objected loudly to the insinuation that their mate wouldn't do it out of devotion to her alone. Silly kitty didn't understand that while Brock smelled like her mate, and looked like her mate, the guy simply was not interested in being her mate.

RAWRR!

Ariella winced. Angry kitty was loud kitty, and

she was still recovering from the whole catnip thing. Her she-Cat needed to tone down her sass.

Sigh.

She could not think about Brock right now. Ariella had other things to worry about. Like the blond mantrap headed her way.

Cornelia Higgins was technically Ariella's second cousin, but their families were not close. Bad blood over one slight or other over the years had led to a little feud between the Higgins and Golden families. As a result, Cornelia had always been a real bitch to Ari and her sisters.

None of them liked her. Still, Ariella had to admit Cornelia was good at her job. Even if she only landed her clients by sleeping with them. Rumors could be nasty things, but these were more like what people called *open secrets.*

"She gives us all a bad name," Toni mumbled as they exited the conference room.

"Why? Because she'd rather gain clients on her knees than with her brains?" Adrianna snarled loudly, and Ari pinched her arm.

Talk like that would only bring Cornelia herself over their way to flaunt her achievements in their faces. The woman loved to brag, and unscrupulous or not, she had the numbers to back it up.

"Well, well, well, if it isn't the *Golden girls*," she said and gave an unfriendly smirk. "Say that show was about a group of old women with no men in their lives, right? Like you four?"

"No, I don't think that's right. After all, one was rather promiscuous," Toni said.

"That means she was a slut, Corny. Kinda like some females we know," Annabeth hissed.

"Oh, so one of them was getting some," replied Cornelia with her perfect upturned nose in the air, making Ari want to gag. "I guess those girls weren't like you four, after all? Seeing as how none of you can get a man, unless you count a canary."

"Watch it," snarled Annabeth, but Toni held her back.

"Anyway, Ariella, I wanted to congratulate you on your attempt to win the quarterly contest. It is too bad, though."

"What's too bad?" Ari asked.

"Well, let's see, this will be my fifth win in a row, and you never even won once, have you? In fact, none of you have, right?"

"Yeah, we know how you won, Corny," murmured Annabeth, but Toni elbowed her to shush up.

"You know, I have to say so far, the new laptop

was my favorite prize. Of course, the deluxe premium smart phone package was great too. The year-long spa treatments went very well. I mean, we all know those are amazing," she said, and looked at the four sisters scathingly.

"Then again, maybe *we* don't do we, ladies? Anyway, I am really going to enjoy winning this year. The week-long vacation for two sounds divine," Cornelia finished and tossed her perfectly flat-ironed blond locks over one slender shoulder.

Skinny beyotch.

"You haven't won it yet," Ariella responded, eyes narrowed and rising to the bait like a freaking amateur.

"Haven't I?" she crinkled her nose and Ari wondered for a moment how she would look with blood gushing out of it.

Rawrrrr.

"You know, I was going to stop by that little Wolf motorcycle bar for dinner tonight," she taunted.

"I wonder what, or should I say *who*, I might find there. Maybe someone looking for a woman with a little experience under her belt. Maybe my next client," Cornelia said, pursing her lips and winking at Ari before she walked away.

Of course, she didn't get far before Annabeth

reached out with her exceptionally long legs and tripped her. Ariella bit her lip to stop her laughter from exploding out of her mouth.

"Hey!"

"Oops, my bad," Annabeth said, fake smile just innocent enough to not raise suspicion.

Ari knew that one was for her, and she was grateful to Annabeth. Shit. She was positively dying on the inside. She couldn't compete against Cornelia's sexual prowess. After all, what if the woman was right?

What if her virginity was just another, even bigger, obstacle between her and Brock? Cornelia had just poked at an open wound, and Ariella did not know if she would recover. Anger, fear, determination warred within her. Should Ariella just give up now? Hand over the prize to Cornelia and slink away with her tail between her legs.

Fuck. No. Rawrrrr.

CHAPTER 7

"Four porterhouses up," Brock yelled over the dull roar of activity that seemed constant in the busy kitchen.

He'd outfitted the space with the best equipment, though the design was simplistic/ Fitting, seeing as how the menu was mainly grilled meat and fish. He kept things orderly, neat, clean, and his staff knew what their jobs entailed. Anyone caught cutting corners, was fired. No second chances.

Some might call him a cruel boss, but he wasn't. Brock simply needed the best from his team. It was what he gave, and what he demanded in return. Being head chef was a dream come true, but it was hard work.

Cooking was the fun part. Menu creation a close

second. He changed it up every few weeks or so, with different side dishes based on availability and what was in season. The core was the same—steaks, chops, filets, fowl, and whole fish. The ingredients were all top quality. But it was the cooking technique that mattered most, in his opinion.

Brock grunted as his assistants sprinted to get food on plates and out to the servers. Having everything run smoothly and efficiently was of the utmost importance, and as such he believed in quick delivery from flame to plate to customer.

No fuss, no delays.

Shifters had extremely sensitive tastes and food left to sit for any amount of time had already started to spoil. No one wanted to prolong that. True, he wasn't classically trained in a culinary school, but he had wandered the world for many years and had a natural eye and a nose for tastes.

In his travels, Brock had picked up a lot from various master chefs and above average kitchen Witches over the years. Dire Wolves aged even slower than most Shifters and supes, though he was nearing seventy, he still had the appearance of a thirty-year-old.

Shit.

He'd begun to feel his age just lately. Watching

Derrick and Lucy make a home for the cub they were expecting over the past few months had been intense, welcomed, and exciting for sure, but Brock had also started to feel envious of his Alpha.

It was not a good feeling. He was a loyal Wolf, and he loved Derrick like a brother. But yeah, he was jealous, he admitted, even if only to himself. Brock wanted that, too. A family. A mate. His mate.

Ariella.

Her name echoed through his mind. The mere thought of her sent his Dire Wolf to growling. The big, almost white Wolf was completely besotted with the feline. That single kiss they'd shared in the cool creek had not been nearly enough. But he would never take advantage of a woman under the influence, and certainly not one who'd fallen unconscious in his arms. No. he was too much a gentleman for that.

He had simply seen her home, safe and sound. Brock wondered if it wasn't kismet that she had passed out before things could progress any further. They weren't there yet. Maybe they wouldn't ever be.

Fuck. He wasn't cut out for a mate. Frolicking in the moonlight was one thing. A stolen kiss, another. But having to subject her to his enormous size when she was untried and innocent, well, that was something else entirely.

What if she panicked and ran from him like Jacqueline had all those years ago?

That one experience was the root of all his anxiety. And yet, Brock wondered, how could the Fates be wrong? Warring arguments sounded loudly in his brain until he was practically vibrating with frustration.

Hell, even their resident Pack spitfire had found a mate. Sheila and Leo were like water and oil, but they made it work. Why couldn't he and Ariella?

He could've gone on being lonely forever, but then Derrick mated Lucy and Sheila mated Leo. He had to admit the Lion was a pretty cool guy for a hard ass cop who was also a Prince. Leo was the reason Brock had met Ariella, who was an honorary cousin of the male.

So, he could say Leo was the cause of all his angst, worry, and the ever-growing feeling that something was missing from his life. The fucker. Brock ran a hand over his face. It didn't matter if Leo was to blame or Sheila, or whoever the fuck. Ariella was fucking worth it.

He recalled the way her soft lips had parted so readily for his. The woman had a mouth made for sin with a sightly plumper upper lip that he wanted to nibble on for days. Her wild curly hair was glorious, a dark halo circling her head. She was beautiful. Perfect.

Mate, his Wolf growled.

Well, fuck.

His dick hardened in his chef pants and Brock was practically vibrating, he was growling so much. He couldn't concentrate. Not like this.

"No more than three minutes to a side on those four inch steaks, Carlo. That meat goes out rare," he grunted and handed his tongs to his new sous chef, a half-Fae kid of about three-hundred years old, who'd decided he wanted to be a chef.

The man looked even younger than Brock, but he worked hard and was never late. Carlo nodded and took over the grill with all the seriousness required for the job. The last thing Brock needed was for some Shifter customer to freak the fuck out over a badly cooked steak.

But he had no reason to worry. He had already worked on the sauces for the rest of the dishes, and his staff knew what they were doing. Brock barked out a few more orders, checking one last time to make sure the fish and veggies were all prepped before he walked out of the kitchen.

He trusted his crew. Knew they could handle the Monday dinner rush with efficiency and professionalism. They were a great team and Cole, one of his Pack, was always there to step in if they got in trouble. Brock simply needed some time to think.

"Chef?" Tim, a new server, and Fox Shifter, came rushing into the small locker room they kept for staff. Brock was sitting there with his eyes closed, trying to calm his inner beast. "There's a woman here to see you."

Brock opened his eyes and his Wolf stilled inside of him, like the predator he admittedly was who had his prey backed into a corner. Ariella, he thought, and took off his apron. He could hardly contain himself as he stalked through the full tables and weaved between folks just standing by the bar.

He'd been waiting ever since Saturday night for her to call him. Where was she? Brock ran a hand over his head and encountered his tied kerchief. He ripped the thing off and tossed it on an empty stool. It didn't matter. He had dozens of the things. It would not matter if he lost one. Whatever. He'd just wanted to look better when he saw her again.

There was nothing he could do about the checked chef pants and black chef coat he still wore, but hey, she knew what he did for a living. She wouldn't have come there expecting anything more. Curiosity got the best of him as he retraced his steps through the dining room and back to the bar once more.

Was she playing some sort of game? He looked over the head of a busty blond who smelled like a flower shop and made his nose itch. The ridiculous woman looked as if she was going to fall over, trying to get his attention.

"Hello there," she said, offering him with what she must have thought was a seductive smile. Brock was not interested. He nodded and continued to look around for Ariella.

"Excuse me, you are the chef, right? Brock Laurent? I'm Cornelia Higgins," she said in a husky voice, and offered a freshly manicured hand. Brock looked down at it, making no move to touch the female.

"Yes, I'm the chef. Did you have a question? I don't have much time, I'm sorry, I am waiting for someone," he replied, gingerly shaking her offered appendage.

He tried to extract himself, but the woman was cloying. She refused to let go.

"Yes, that would be me," she replied to his utter

confusion, using his momentary lapse as an excuse to push her slender body against his.

What the hell was going on? Where was Ariella? Brock looked through the sparse crowd, but she was nowhere to be found.

"Excuse me, I don't think so," he returned, putting space between them, and tugging his hand free of hers none too gently.

He knew she was a Shifter, having scented her fur, which was why he thought it strange she would be so forward. Shifters, especially powerful ones like Dire Wolves, did not like to be touched unless it was invited. Brock was definitely not interested in her hands anywhere near him.

"I asked the server to go get you."

"What? Why?"

"Well, it is your lucky day, Mr. Laurent," she started and grinned again, not put off in the slightest that he was less than welcoming. "I'm here to meet the famous chef of the newest Blue Valley hotspot, and to give you the deal of your dreams."

"Yeah, look, there has been a mistake. I'm busy," he said and turned to walk away, but the woman grabbed his arm, and it was all he could do to keep still.

His Wolf was snarling. The beast did not want this female to touch him. He hated it.

"Maybe I was not being clear enough. I'm Cornelia Higgins and I represent *Eat Well Live Proud*, Mr. Laurent. I am completely at your service," she said and emphasized the service part by tracing every line of his body with her eyes.

Brock stiffened, repulsed by her overly suggestive comments and too intimate glances. He stepped back, away from her grasp. He wasn't a fan of this Lioness and could tell from the start she meant trouble. He quirked an eyebrow and turned to see Weylin wander over. He was bartending tonight.

"Need something, bro?" Weylin asked.

"Miss Higgins?" he questioned out of courtesy only.

"I will have a white wine," she replied and seemed quite pleased with herself.

"I'll have a mineral water," he told Weylin.

"I have been dying to meet the genius behind Serious Moonlight's innovative menu, and now that I have," she began, her eyes roaming over him again, making him squirm uncomfortably. "I can tell this deal is going to be my pleasure entirely. I don't normally offer our exclusive meat line to just anyone, you know."

Brock was feeling like a piece of meat himself. He even backed up, putting a stool between them, pointing towards the glass of wine Weylin set down on the bar before she could stand and follow him.

Sheesh, get a hint, lady.

Cornelia's offer was basic. She wanted to move their account to *her* management and give him the *personal attention* he was presumably missing. But Brock had already stopped listening. A familiar, delicious musk seemed to float across the room and wrap around him. He recognized the scent. It belonged to the only person he was interested in handling his accounts.

Clearly, Miss Higgins was used to conducting business in a certain manner—*like on her back.* Something he would never pursue, especially not with her. Not even in the slightest. There was only one feline he was interested in.

As if on cue, Ariella Golden chose that moment to walk in. Cornelia droned on, clearly delusional. Her badly veiled innuendos were obvious, and cliché. Her intent to seal the deal with a night in the sack was distasteful to both him and his Wolf.

As if he would ever be interested in her. But the idea did get him thinking. He turned his head and met Ariella's large amber eyes. They glowed gold with her Lioness for a moment as she seemed to take in the situation before she turned and left.

Oh, that wouldn't do. Not at all.

"Excuse me, Miss Higgins, you seem to be operating under the misinformation that we don't have an account handler with Eat Well Live Proud, which I am sure if you looked, you would see we do, with Ariella Golden. Secondly, you seem to think I would be interested in you sexually, and you are using that imagined sexual interest to misguide you. If you came here thinking I would take you up on your offer to sleep with you in exchange for our business, well, you are grossly mistaken. The answer is no," he said and moved to leave.

Unfortunately, what Cornelia Higgins lacked in scruples, she made up for in speed. The wily feline stood in front of him and placed a hand over the semi-hard erection in his pants.

"I think you look and feel plenty interested. This is really quite the package you have here, Mr. Laurent. Better to go with a woman who knows how to handle it then some virgin who might faint on sight," Cornelia said, biting her lip and blinking up at him with the same practiced look she must have given dozens of men.

Of course, his semi-hard state was pretty much

the norm for whenever Ariella was in the same zip code as him. It had nothing whatsoever to do with this aggressive female. She grinned again, gave his cock another squeeze, angering both him and his Wolf.

Brock growled and removed her hand with perhaps a tad bit more force than necessary. She was a Shifter, and quite strong. The fact she had attacked his one area of weakness aside, Brock could see Cornelia had issues of her own. Unfortunately for her, he didn't care one whit for them. His concern was for Ariella alone.

"I am not interested in you or your offer, Miss Higgins. I can't say it any plainer than that. You see, I've found my fated mate. Now, I will say this once and only once—Do. Not. Touch. Me. Ever. Again."

Cornelia gasped at whatever she saw in his gaze and backed up rubbing her hands Together. He would have felt guilty, but she was too damn pushy and needed the reality check.

"B-but what about the deal? There's a quarterly contest and the prize is an island vacation. I intend to win it. If you help me, you can be my plus one, Mr. Laurent."

"A contest? You would spread your legs for a man

who clearly is not interested, for a contest? No deal, Ms. Higgins, and I suggest you get some help."

"How dare you! Look, I will overlook your lack of taste, but if I have your account then—"

"I already said we have a rep. If you want to win something, I suggest you work harder. Now, I suggest you leave and don't come back, Ms. Higgins."

Brock turned around and chased the enticing trail of musk and spice that Ariella had left in her wake. Shit, that encounter took too long. Was he too late?

He jogged, then ran out the side door. Fuck. Where was she? The sun had already set for the evening, and it was dark and chilly in the Spring breeze. The sound of leaves rustling caught his attention, and he rounded the back, searching behind the small outdoor storage closet. Another rustle of leaves and branches sounded, and he stepped into the woods where Brock's eyes zeroed in on the most beautiful thing he'd ever seen.

Ariella Golden stood in her skin and nothing else. Her eyes flashed at him, and she hissed angrily before changing into her fierce and magnificent Lioness. Her shift was fast, though not as fast as his. The sound of bones cracking and muscles reknitting themselves was loud in the back of the restaurant, but he understood. She was upset and it was his fault.

The she-Cat roared before sprinting off into the woods and Brock grinned. He wasn't leaving well enough alone. Not tonight. If a chase was what she wanted, she was about to get one. He ran towards the stand of trees where the glorious golden feline had just disappeared. Without a thought for his clothing, he called his Dire Wolf forward.

After decades of shifting, his change was instantaneous. His animal was enormous, far larger than the average Wolf Shifter, and he had light, buff-colored fur that was almost white on his chest and face and darkest on his back. In his Wolf form, all of his senses seemed to increase tenfold. Including, his sense of smell.

The intoxicating fragrance coming from his mate was almost overwhelming. He didn't need to see or hear her to find her, he just had to follow his nose.

He loosed a howl and sprinted after her. All his earlier fears about their mating forgotten when he was in his fur. The beast had no such qualms, knowing in his heart that he was the perfect mate for his sweet kitten.

Brock's Wolf growled with the knowledge that he was the only male in the entire universe who could give her everything she could ever need or want. It was why he was born, after all, to be Ariella's mate.

Mating fever.

The thought crashed into him as his stomach tightened and he pumped his legs faster, straining his muscles to catch up to her. The pull of the near full moon was making his desire even stronger.

Hell, he felt it in his very soul. The strength of his need for her was undeniable. Brock tossed his lupine head back and sniffed good and long.

This way.

The sound of leaves and twigs snapping under his massive paws only fed his predatory instincts. He had to reach her. His Wolf knew she was upset, that she had misinterpreted what she'd seen, and he was pissed as hell at Brock for not pushing the other woman off immediately. But that was to be expected, mates were often very possessive of one another, and his animal's nature didn't always follow or approve of his human side's need to act with a certain degree of civility.

Things like manners and decorum were not important to a Dire Wolf. He had to make it right, to prove that she was his one and only. The sound of a splash caught his attention, and he turned right.

Was she headed back to their stream?

Seemed like his kitty wanted to go for a swim. Brock's Wolf howled once more into the night air before he took off in that direction. His sassy little mate had no idea what was coming for her.

Game on.

CHAPTER 8

Ariella couldn't believe her Lioness right now! She wanted to hightail it out of the parking lot, but her beast decided she needed her fur now.

Ugh.

As if that was not bad enough—Miss Kitty ran right back to the scene of Ari's abject humiliation. As if she hadn't had enough of that.

Ugh.

The little creek behind the Dire Wolf Pack House was just as clear and chilly as her fuzzy memory recollected. She chuffed as she vaulted into the invigorating water. Her feline side figured it was worth a try. Maybe she could forget about her sorrows with an energizing swim. But Cornelia Higgins? Did it have to be her?

She just could not believe her own eyes. Seeing that female with her hands on him sent Ari on a downward spiral that had her shedding her clothes in the woods not twenty feet from the crowded roadhouse.

Rawrr.

Sure, he had walked outside and caught her. But he was not there for Ari. No way would she even entertain that line of thought. Brock had probably been getting his bike ready, so he could follow Cornelia to her den of carnal delights.

That Wolf didn't want a virginal mate any more than she wanted to be a virgin. Good for him, getting his rocks off with a born seductress. Ariella couldn't seduce her way out of a traffic ticket.

Sigh.

Wasn't that the embarrassing truth? Her unfortunately timed announcement that she was untouched, *and therefore unwanted,* ruined any chance she could have had at playing the siren. She should just give up and move far away from Blue Valley and the Pride already.

If only she had beaten Cornelia to the roadhouse. If only she had beaten Cornelia, period. Then she could have stopped that woman's come ons before they'd happened. Darn it.

Rawrrrr.

Winning the contest was important to Ariella, but it was nothing when she compared it to claiming her mate. But Brock was simply unattainable. And Ari never flirted with clients. She would never sleep her way to the top. It just was not her style. Rumors about Cornelia's unsavory ways had been circulating for months. But Ari was naïve, she supposed. She simply could not fathom it. She had worked hard for every single one of her accounts.

It wasn't slut-shaming or woman-hating that made her lip curl at the thought of Cornelia coming on to Brock. Having a hearty appetite for sex was all fine and good, but why did the woman have to go after him? The fact she was using her body to land accounts was none of Ariella's business.

Though, it was probably against company policy. She really had no shame about it, either. The woman flaunted it to everyone at EWLP. There was a code of ethics they were all supposed to follow, but Ari did not have them memorized or anything.

Still, she doubted Cornelia's activities were kosher. And the way the female bragged and made fun of the women and men who refused to conduct business in that manner was just horrid. Cornelia was like a walking, talking throwback to some shady businesswoman stereotype, and Ariella would never use her methods to build her client list like that, nor did she want that kind of reputation.

To Ari, intimacy was supposed to be *intimate*. As in personal, between two people who had mutual respect and feelings for one another. Probably why she was still a virgin.

Sad rawr.

The leaves stirred, and her leonine eyes took in the beauty of the forest. She was lucky to live in this place. New Jersey was known, and ridiculed, for its highways, but it had some of the prettiest woods she'd ever seen. From beaches, to mountains, farmland, and cities. It had a little bit of everything. Or, as her mom said, something for everyone—though the Lioness might have been talking about the food court at the new mall down on Route 35 at the time.

Anyway, it was obvious to her Brock didn't care for her shy and private nature. Maybe he wanted someone who was more an exhibitionist. Like Cornelia. He sure looked fine and cozy chatting with her at the bar.

Sad sad rawr.

Ariella exited the stream and laid her big furry body out on a large bolder on the bank. The enormous rock was still warm from the afternoon sun.

She was soaked but felt better now, calmer, and relaxed after her swim. She closed her eyes for a catnap but was startled by a huge splash.

The cold water shocked her into standing up. She turned her head to see an enormous white Wolf swimming across the stream to where she lay. Ariella hissed loudly at the male invading her space. She just wanted to be alone, dammit.

Taking a deep breath, she caught the Wolf's scent and recognized it immediately. Heart pounding, her hiss turned into a purr as the Wolf neared her.

Brock.

Her *would-be-mate*, who, according to her calculations, should be at second base with Cornelia by now, was headed straight for her. Before she could talk herself out of it, she switched fur for skin without bothering to care about her nudity.

Most Shifters had grown up around that kind of thing, and she was too amped up to be properly embarrassed by her fleshy thighs and soft belly. Why was he here? She just had to know, and supernatural or not, she could not talk in her fur.

"What are you doing here?" she asked as he climbed to shore and shook out his fur, shifting back to his skin at the same time.

"I came to talk to you," he said and continued to

shake his head in a manner that reminded her of his animal.

She couldn't help but smile as her eyes followed the movement. Ari bit her lip, her gaze wandering over him in a manner that was decidedly against Shifter protocol.

Fuck it.

Ariella felt entitled. She'd spent so much time imagining the moment the two of them were naked together, she might as well take advantage. If pressed, she could always argue she was helpless in his presence. It was not a lie.

Gulp. Beautiful, sexy, muscly man.

Her eyes devoured every inch of him from the top of his damp blond hair to his wide shoulders, amazing pecs, rippling abs, and lower still. Mouth open, she flat out stared in shock as she reached that large, unfamiliar part of him that seemed to grow, jutting out proudly from its bed of damp blond curls.

"Ariella, if you don't stop looking at me like that, this conversation is going to be a short one," he growled softly, and she noted his eyes glowing blue with his Wolf.

If Ariella didn't know any better, she would think he was desperately trying to keep control. Imagine that? The big, gorgeous hunk of man was having a hard time keeping a lid on his Wolf because of her. That knowledge was incredibly empowering, and she tucked it away like a secret she would keep with her always.

If Ari was staring, then so was he. His bold gaze roamed up and down her curves, and she felt damp heat pool between her legs. Need and desire rose like the tide, and she swayed on her feet. Throwing caution to the wind, Ariella stepped over to where he stood, encroaching on his personal space. She noted with delight the way his eyes dropped to her swaying breasts and lower to the carefully cropped curls that shielded her sex from his piercing gaze.

So, he isn't as immune as he pretended to be. Good to know.

"So, you wanted to talk?" she asked, stopping inches shy from touching his body. She gestured for him to get on with it.

"Is it true that there is an employee contest at *Eat Well Live Proud?*"

"What?"

Ariella was confused. What kind of question was that? It had nothing to do with anything. Here she was tingling with want and he was asking about work.

What. The. Actual. Fuck.

"Is it true?" he reiterated.

"Yes," she replied cautiously.

"Where are you in the running?"

"Why do you want to know?" she asked.

"Because," he returned vaguely. "Just tell me."

"Okay, yes, there is a contest, and right now I am tied for first with your new friend," she emphasized the word and crossed her arms.

"That woman is not my friend. I just met her tonight. She wants my business," he began, a cocky grin splitting his face. "And that wasn't all she wanted."

"I bet," she huffed.

A burning jealousy built inside of her, the same feeling that had Ariella running out of the bar earlier and shifting into her she-Cat. She couldn't stop the hiss that escaped her throat at the mention of Cornelia. Lucky for that beyotch, Ariella had some sense of decorum, otherwise she'd have ripped her hair out.

"I turned her down," he added, watching her closely.

"Why?"

"Because I wanted to offer it to you. The same deal she offered me."

"What do you mean?"

"I mean you will have *all* of Serious Moonlight's business, if—"

"Really? You will go all in for our beef, lamb, wild game, poultry, and ALL of our seafood products?" she asked and bounced on the balls of her feet in her excitement.

She stopped the second she heard his growl, his eyes glued to her swaying breasts. Ariella cleared her throat, fighting the burning blush she felt creeping up her face. It was gratifying he was finally noticing her as a woman. Maybe they could spend time together and get to know each other. That would be amazing.

If Brock got to know her, maybe he would like her and eventually, they could come to some kind of an understanding. So lost in her fantasy, Ariella could not believe his next few words. Maybe she did not hear him correctly.

"I'm sorry, what did you say?" she asked, blinking up at him.

"I said, you can have all our business, Ariella, if you agree to stay on as our rep with Eat Well Live Proud, and if you agree to spend the night with me."

Ariella's mouth hung open. Could he mean what she thought he meant? His proposition echoed in her head. His offer filtering through her lust-addled brain. Brock Laurent was finally admitting he wanted her, but only for a night.

Yessss, hissed her she-Cat.

No, replied her brain.

How could she live with herself if she gave him her body to use for the night? Well, at least she could say she had him, right? This was an impossible choice.

Fuck.

She was frozen solid. Ariella could hardly breathe as her entire world came crashing down around her head. This was too big, too important to decide right now. Her heart constricted in her chest and her lungs threatened to seize up as breathing suddenly became difficult.

"Um, *er,* I'll call you later with my decision," she said and turned away from him, unwilling to have him witness the myriad of emotions racing through her.

Did he think all the women from EWLP were for sale, like Cornelia? Did he simply have no respect for her? She wished she could be outraged, but mostly she was confused. And if she were being honest, she was intrigued as well.

"Ariella?" he called, but she didn't turn around,

just raised her hand as she walked towards Pride lands.

"I need to think, Brock. Call me later, and you'll have your answer."

"Fine. But I will call, Ariella."

She nodded, uncertain whether that was a good thing. Swallowing down her shock, she made plans to call her sisters. It was time for a Golden girls meeting.

Rawrrr.

CHAPTER 9

"You're a fucking idiot," Derrick, his Alpha and best friend, said and tossed back a shot of Mason Lane's newest artisan distilled whiskey, *Peanut Butter Bite.*

The dark-haired Alpha nodded at Phoenix, who then added a few cases of the liquor to their regular order. It was bound to be a hit with canid Shifters and Pachyderms who frequented the place.

How normals never caught on to Shifters was a mystery to Brock, but whatever. He supposed most people only saw what they wanted to see.

"You know, if you chase that with this *Jersey Devil's Brewery Sour Raspberry* ale, it's like eating a PB&J," Phoenix remarked and wagged his eyebrows.

"Great. Put it on the cocktail specials for this

month," Derrick said to him, then turned to nod at Brock.

"Phoenix, what do you think of this idiot over here?"

"Oh, he's fucked," Phoenix said.

The Wolf grinned, ducked and reached a hand upward, plucking the shot glass Brock threw at his head from out of the air. Weylin and Thor were busy picking up supplies in town, and Cole had left a few days ago for a ride.

Out of all of them, he'd been having the hardest time adjusting to life off the road, so they all understood when he needed to get gone.

"Fuck you," Brock retorted, then dropped his head in his hands.

He didn't know where he'd gotten the brilliant idea to proposition his mate, but it was all he could think of to save them both from the horrifying possibility that he was simply too much for her to handle.

Like Jacqueline.

His Wolf snarled at the hated memory.

"Shit, Derrick. What am I gonna do? She must think I'm a fucking asshole, man," he growled.

"Yes, and she would be right."

His Alpha smirked annoyingly. Fucking asshole.

But that was not true. Brock knew Derrick for a long time, and the man was as good as they came. He cared about their Pack and was a great leader.

"Look," Derrick said, taking pity on him, thank fuck. "Do you love her?"

"Love? I don't know," Brock replied, cocking his head to the side as if he'd never considered the possibility. Fuck. Did he love her?

"Well, how do you feel about her, man?"

"I want her like crazy. I mean, Ariella is all I think about. She's my fated mate, Derrick. There is no doubt. I can feel it in my blood. My Wolf knows it, The beast wants her. But what does that have to do with love?"

"Have you learned nothing from me and Lucy? It has everything to do with it. I mean, look, the pull to mate was so strong, I nearly claimed her in the first ten minutes of meeting her. But love followed immediately after, too. I swear, every minute I spend with my mate, I love her even more."

"Ew, man, cut that shit out," Phoenix grunted and made a face at the two men. "Sappy motherfucking shit might be contagious."

"Hell, you'd be lucky! Besides, you're going to have a long wait for someone to take on your sorry ass," Derrick rumbled and tossed a rag in his Pack mate's face.

They continued their ribbing as their Alpha moved on to the next shot. He passed a second glass to Brock. He sniffed the Vanilla Bourbon liquor they'd just received from a Gator Shifter family down in Kentucky.

It was good stuff, Brock acknowledged as he took in the smoky depths of the bronze-colored liquid and sniffed it for hints of oak and sugar. The color reminded him of Ariella's eyes. That haunted expression she wore as she had left the woods last night, had almost been his undoing.

Fuck.

Was everything going to remind him about her from now on? He had yet to call her. Truth was, he'd chickened out. Again.

"Look, bro, I know you have some hang ups, but she's a Shifter man. Not some human who isn't prepared for the ferocity of your ardor. She is not Jacqueline. Ariella can more than handle anything you got," Derrick said point blank.

He spoke in a low voice out of respect for the sensitivity of the discussion, and Brock's Wolf appreciated the consideration. He wanted to believe him. Really, he did.

"Call her or I will fucking order you to," Derrick said before turning back to his task.

"Alright," Brock replied.

There was no holding back now. He had to do it before he lost his chance and she walked away from him for good. He stood up and walked a few feet away, trying to find his balls. Grabbing his cell phone, he dialed her number and waited while it rang.

"Hello."

"Hey," he answered.

Relief filled him so quickly it was dizzying. Brock realized he hadn't been sure she would even deem him worthy enough to answer his call.

"Brock?" she asked when he said nothing for more than a beat, and he snapped himself out of his stupor.

"Yeah. It's me."

"I know. I have caller id."

"Ariella, I wanted to talk about what I said last night—"

"My answer is yes."

"What? You're saying yes? Are you sure—"

He could hardly believe what she was saying.

"Yes, Brock, I will spend one night with you, and in return you'll sign the contract for Eat Well Live Proud to

be the sole supplier of meat and fish for Serious Moonlight."

"Ariella, are you certain?"

"Yes, I am sure. See you at eight tonight, alright?"

"Eight o'clock. Alright."

"Alright, then."

He waited for her to end the call, then turned around and slid the phone back into his pocket. Now he was the one who was confused. Ariella had agreed to spend the night with him. He knew she was a virgin. Knew what he'd asked was stupid and cruel.

Why would she agree to it, though?

"She said yes?" Derrick's voice raised an octave as if he was just as baffled as his Beta.

Brock nodded. He was lost for words. Of course, his Dire Wolf was completely on board with getting Ariella to bed him any way he could. Maybe it would work out, maybe it wouldn't. But one thing he knew, he couldn't fuck this up again.

He had to come clean and tell her the truth. He'd been running from her because of a bad experience from his past, punishing her for the sins of another. It was petty and stupid.

But one night? Was she serious? He had to hope and pray she'd commit to more than a night. Fuck, once he had her, his Dire Wolf would never let her go. He knew that with a certainty he wasn't altogether familiar with. It was more than the beast, though. Brock couldn't picture walking away from her.

Could Derrick be right? Was he in love with the lovely Lioness after all?

"Chest hurt?"

Derrick interrupted his thoughts and Brock looked down to see he was rubbing the center of his chest with his palm. He nodded at his Alpha.

"Yeah," he said, and tilted his head to the side, waiting for an explanation.

He felt like a fucking cub. Completely at sea in the vast ocean that was the complexity of his feelings for the woman. Derrick motioned for him to sit and continued.

"Find yourself confused a lot lately? Anxious when she isn't near?"

Again Brock nodded. How did Derrick know about that?

"Capable of hammering through a concrete wall with your cock whenever she is close?"

"Yes," Brock growled unhappily.

The Alpha chuckled. This was not the shit he wanted to talk about with another man. But Derrick was more than that. He was their chosen leader. Trust and loyalty were only two of the emotions he felt for the male.

Derrick was a good man and an awesome leader. Their bond as Beta and Alpha made their relationship a strong one. If he couldn't talk to him, who could he?

"Then the answer is simple. You are royally fucked, son, because yes, she is your fated mate, and yes, even if you did not realize it, you're already halfway in love with her."

"Why half?"

"Have you kissed her properly yet?"

Brock shook his head, and ignored the fact that his cheeks were burning, and were probably bright red. He felt like a fucking idiot. He had kissed her once, but it was not nearly thorough enough to suit his feelings for her.

"The second you do, your Wolf will want to gut you from the inside out if you don't stake your claim and mark that woman for the rest of your lives. The desire you feel now is nothing to how you will feel after you give her your bite."

"It gets worse?" Brock scowled.

What the fuck? Was he doomed to walk around a slave to this woman for all time?

Yesss, the Wolf inside him growled. *And it will be the best fucking thing we could ever hope for.*

"Son, you don't know the half of it, but if you're lucky, she'll let you claim her and then she'll claim your sorry ass right back. Best fucking time of my life, having Lucy bite the shit out of me. I'd die for that woman, Brock. Even scarier, I'd kill for her. Do terrible things to keep her safe and happy. She knows it too, and her love for me is a bottomless well. I can feel it in our bond. I am a lucky bastard," Derrick rumbled.

They clinked glasses and took the next shot, this one was a new brand of tequila that went down smoothly. Brock turned his shot glass upside down and sat looking at his hands with Derrick by his side, enjoying the silence. Of course, it did not last long.

Both men turned as the side door to the bar came swinging open and a very pregnant Lucy came strolling through with bags on each arm and a rosy, pink glow to her cheeks. Her belly seemed to enter the roadhouse a step before the rest of her body, and he felt Derrick tense in his seat next to him. The Alpha stood already on his way to her side, but Phoenix beat him there, taking her burdens from her hands and leaving her free to greet her mate.

"Hey boys, come help me," she said when she

entered, and Phoenix nodded, already heading out to the car to unload her goodies.

Derrick was already across the floor and lifting her up in his arms for their usual hello kiss and embrace. Normally, the others turned away out of respect, but this time Brock watched and what he saw fascinated him.

The couple nuzzled each other softly, whispering words he couldn't quite make out before kissing one another. When they connected, it was like their entire bodies glowed with the soft ethereal light of their matebond. The two of them fucking oozed love, and for the first time ever, Brock admitted he wanted that for himself.

Not with Lucy, or Derrick, for that matter—but with Ariella.

He wanted her to accept his claim. To share her life with him. To have a strong matebond. To make a family.

Now, he just had to convince her.

―――

At eight PM, he pulled up to her apartment, noting the large lion statues on either side of the lobby's main entrance. Brock rolled his eyes in exasperation. Leave it to a bunch of cat Shifters to emulate themselves in stone for all to see.

SMH.

His Wolf growled inside his mind's eye. But Brock simply smirked and walked up the stairs. Ariella's apartment was on the second floor. She had offered to meet him outside, but he wanted to treat this like the real date it was, especially after having fucked up so royally.

A dozen long-stemmed red roses in hand, Brock walked down the hall to her door, and pulled on the jacket of his custom tux. It was his, not rented, as he needed it tailored for his extra-large frame. He'd combed back his longish blond hair, scrubbed himself from head to toe in the shower, and even shaved his facial hair for the occasion. He'd wanted to look his best for what he had planned.

Brock rang the bell and waited with bated breath for her to answer. Even then, he was unprepared for the sight that met his eyes. Holy hell. She was drop dead gorgeous. The personification of every dream, *wet and otherwise,* he'd ever had.

He swallowed loudly as Ariella stood at the door. Her golden eyes, while contemplative at first, filled with delight as he held out his meager offering. Meager compared to her. She wore a deep red gown, hugging her generous curves, embracing, and caressing them like a lover's hands, and he had half a mind to tear the thing off.

Was it possible to be jealous of clothes? Well, he was. He managed not to rip it from her skin—barely. The confection ended mid-calf, but his gaze traveled lower, paying attention to the slit revealing her smooth thigh, supple calf, slender ankle, and down to the pair of strappy red high-heeled shoes completing the ensemble. Damn outfit should've been illegal. Probably was in some places.

Brock had always been a sucker for women in heels, and the ones she had on were spiked and sexy and made him want to drop to his knees and worship at her feet. Her dark curls floated around her shoulders like a velvet cloud and he was tempted to run his fingers through it, but he knew better than to touch a woman's hair without invitation.

Later, he told himself, and handed her the roses.

A deep breath told him she had company, but he wasn't worried about it. They were her family. Still, it nagged at him. They probably thought he'd propositioned her for an evening. Soon enough, the record would be set straight.

"Thank you," she said shyly, placing the vase of flowers on the table.

"You said to dress up," she spoke in a breathless whisper of a voice that shot sparks of electricity right to his cock. "Is this okay?"

"Yes. It's perfect," he said with pure honesty.

His Wolf made his voice gravelly, and he cleared his throat before he continued, feeling much like a pup on his first date. In effect, he was.

"Shall we?" Brock offered Ariella his arm and felt ten feet tall when she placed her small hand in the crook of his elbow so trustingly.

He'd put her in a bad position, yet still, she trusted him. The thought was humbling, and he thanked the gods for the blessing she truly was in his life. Emotion filled him to the brink. Thunder roared in his ears and his chest was damn near to exploding. He knew then Derrick had been right.

I love her.

Fuck, yes, he did. He was head over heels for Ariella Golden. The acknowledgement burst a dam inside of him. Brock felt better than he had in weeks. She smiled up at him shyly, and fuck, he felt it down to his toes. She was more important than anything else had ever been in his whole life.

Loving her was easy, he realized. If he was lucky, Brock would get to do it for a very long time.

Mine.

CHAPTER 10

arlier that evening...

Ariella's pulse raced, and her heart was hammering inside her chest. She couldn't believe her own mother and sisters had talked her into accepting Brock's insane proposal.

If only it was a proposal, her Lioness lamented.

Sad rawr.

The head over heels she-Cat wanted to use the upcoming night as an excuse to claim her mate, but Ariella had absolutely shut that plan down. Either Brock didn't know she was his mate, or he didn't care. Either way, she was not biting him.

Besides, wouldn't her fated mate know who she was and want her above all others? She felt a pang of sadness at the thought he could simply leave her after a night. It was almost worth her calling off the whole thing.

But her she-Cat couldn't stand the idea of any other male getting near her, and this might be her only chance to experience carnal bliss. Winning the contest with *Serious Moonlight's* contract might provide a balm of sorts for the future, she reasoned, even though the prospect of trading sex for his signature left a bad taste in her mouth.

Ariella didn't want to die a spinster. Not like her poor Aunt Alicia, who had died only last year. Poor woman had never found a man to look beyond her ample ass, or so her mother said whenever her unfortunate sister's name was brought up.

Maybe this was her shot to change his mind?

"Easy girl," Patricia Golden grunted as she'd zipped up the scarlet red gown Ariella had bought on impulse months ago, but never had the nerve to wear.

"That puppy doggy of yours is gonna flip his lid when he sees you in this!"

"Hell, yeah, you look all juicy and red like a strawberry ice pop!" Adrianna giggled.

Ariella looked down at herself and groaned. The ensemble was super tight and so over the top she couldn't imagine why she had bought it in the first place.

Ugh.

But it was love at first sight and she'd put it on her credit card and kept it tucked away in her closet. Even the months she'd spent paying off the ridiculous thing would prove worth it if Brock fell head over heels for her after tonight.

"Are you sure I should wear this one?"

"Am I sure? This little number practically screams *gimme your eggplant emoji.* You just listen to your mother, and you will bag yourself a puppy tonight! Just remember honey, we she-Cats mark in two ways, with teeth and claw. You just scratch him, and that doggy is all yours. Get 'em!" Her mother slapped her on her butt and spun her around to face the mirror.

"Mom! Ohmygawd! Is that me?"

"Mom's wight, Awi," Annabeth said with a mouthful of snacks. *"You wook gweat! Hank agwees, I sent him a pwic."*

Her sister's exuberance for her outfit was followed by some serious *nom nom noming.* Good thing Ariella spoke fluent *Lioness-with-mouth-full.* She rolled her eyes and covered her face with her hands.

This whole thing was borderline insane. Ariella's shock when Brock had made his indecent, and yet exciting, proposal had basically caused her brain to shut down. Her hormones were going into overdrive.

Panicked and shocked, she had to leave the woods, and him, just to clear her mind. On the verge of fucking up her life, she did the only thing she could think of. She'd run home to her mother and found her and all of her sisters having a good old time with her last bottle of tequila and the new bag of chips and jar of mango jalapeno salsa she'd brought home the night before.

"Those chips were mine," she whined.

"Come on, sugar," her mother said.

She'd dragged her up in a big mom style hug, and Ari had poured out the whole sob story. Her sisters commiserated and made Ari a plate and a mango margarita on the rocks with a sugared rim—her favorite cocktail—while they hatched a plan.

"Are the drinks laced?" Ariella had wisely asked.

"Nope," Annabeth said, and shook her head, dislodging some crumbs from her otherwise lovely face.

She was staying the night since her mate was out taking his favorite client on a cross-country ride.

Hank, Annabeth's mate, owned a limo service company. He was a decent guy, even if his Shifter animal was an overrated parakeet—a constant point of contention between Annabeth and her Lioness family. Of course, they were only kidding. Mostly.

Whatever. Everyone knows Cats rule.

"You sure about this, sis?" Adrianna asked, handing her a shot glass full of liquid courage.

"I am," she sighed, and turned to look at three pairs of similar golden eyes.

"I love him. He's my mate, and this is my only chance to show him that. Now, what about this drink? Was Mom anywhere near it?"

"Oh, sweetie," Adrianna said, ignoring her question. Her sister sniffed and blew air kisses at her. "I can't believe you found your mate!"

"Oh, he hasn't agreed to let me claim him, but maybe after tonight," she said and bit her lip, her uncertainty growing by the second.

"Look, we confiscated Mom's catnip yesterday. But if you need some?" Toni inquired and narrowed her eyes, but Ari shook her head.

"I will be okay without it."

"Good, because you look amazing. Now for some dirt, after we got here last night, King Donovan called and Mom went a little nutso," Toni whispered while their Mom went to the other room to grab Ariella's wrap.

"I swear, I don't know what he did, but she was seriously pissed."

"Yeah, lucky we were here to cheer her up with 'ritas," Annabeth replied and smiled widely, looking more like the Cheshire cat than the Lioness she was.

"Oh no, I wonder what's going on between those two?"

"Beats me, but the rumor is he isn't ready to move on—"

"Here it is!" Patricia announced, waving the shimmery wrap around.

"What is going on? You know, I can smell gossip a mile away, and I will not have it about me or the leader of our Pride."

"But Mom, maybe we can help?" Ariella asked.

"You can't. It's over between me and the King, but we will still respect him and not give in to petty gossip. Now, Ari, drink that shot, and then put this on, and fix your lipstick," she instructed.

"Yeah, then explain this whole thing from the top," Toni said.

So Ariella did as she was told. Mostly. She placed the wrap on the back of the chair. Took the shot.

Fixed her lipstick. Then, she told her family Brock's proposal one last time.

"Lucky dog!"

"Good for you, sweetie."

"About time you get laid."

Varying degrees of acceptance and teasing followed. After offering her comfort and support, the kind only mothers and sisters could give, they all agreed she should accept and then bag the Wolf!

Ariella still didn't know if it was the right thing or not, but here she was dressed and ready.

Ding dong.

"He's here!" squealed Patricia Golden, and with that, she grabbed Ari's sisters by the hems of their shirts and dragged them out of the room.

"Have a good time, honey! Be adventurous," she whisper-screamed.

Ariella knew they could hear and probably see everything from their spots on the floor behind the kitchen island, but she needed them there. They were her support system, no matter how nutty and unconventional.

Opening the door and seeing him standing there, like some tall, gorgeous Prince Charming to her, very unlikely, and a little bit chubby Cinderella, made her smile like a loon.

But this is no fairy tale.

Ariella had to repeat that several times as he led her to a gorgeous, low slung, luxury sports car that she hadn't even realized he owned.

"This is beautiful," she said as he helped her get inside.

"Yes. Very beautiful," his gravelly voice seemed to strike a chord deep within her and she looked up to see his eyes were on her, and not the car at all.

"Where are we going?" she asked after they had been driving for a few minutes and he hadn't given her a single hint.

"Oh, uh, we're going to the cabin," he returned, and she frowned.

A cabin? Why was she so dressed up then? Ariella quirked an eyebrow as they flew past the sign that read *Exiting Blue Valley*. Wherever they were going, she sure hoped she was ready for what was coming.

"Do you like music?"

"Who me?" she asked and noted the playful curl of his lip as he waited for her response. "Sure. I mean, yes, of course."

"This is a demo from one of the bands who recently auditioned for the bar. I think they're good," he murmured and tapped the display screen to play songs across blue tooth from his smart phone to the car.

The music wasn't exactly rock, but it wasn't country either. It was something in between and had a great chorus and melody that made the listener want to move with the beat. The singer's voice was deep and clear, and Ariella liked it right away.

"Is it okay?"

He seemed to care about her answer, so she nodded and smiled. They chatted a little, about the weather, the car, nothing important, but it helped her nerves. When she shivered slightly at the brush of his hand against her thigh as he switched gears, he reacted by turning the heat on for her. It was sweet and thoughtful. Two words she would've never associated with the typically hotheaded chef.

"We're here," he said, and she was surprised to see they had been driving for an hour.

But wherever *here* was, it didn't seem like they'd arrived. She looked out the window at the dark woods rounding them, which only seemed to be lit by the glowing, nearly full moon.

"Where?" she asked as Brock turned down a narrow lane that had suddenly appeared and seemed hidden off the regular traffic route.

That tiny road suddenly gave way to a much

larger two-way intersection and an enormous parking lot. Beyond that was a large building that would in no way cause Ariella to think the word *cabin,* and yet, there it was in large blue letters over the enormous entrance.

This was not a rustic shack in the woods—thank fuck. It was a resort of some kind, snug in the woods off the parkway past Blue Valley. *The Cabin,* she read the sign again. Ariella wondered how she had never heard of this, *judging from the number of cars,* obvious hot spot.

"What is this place?"

"Well, have you ever heard of Stein Luxury Hotel & Resorts?"

"Yes, I mean that's a Shifter run hotel chain. Some of their smaller locations have started ordering products through EWLP."

"Yes, but they are not strictly Shifter. Frank employs all supernatural creatures in his global hotels and resorts, catering to our kind while keeping under the radar. This one is pretty new. Opened for just a month."

"Wow. They built this in a month?"

"Yes, well, like I said, Mr. Stein is not averse to hiring any supernatural beings, and it's been said he dabbles in magical arts," he shrugged.

"You mean like Witchcraft?"

"You can turn into a Lioness, love, and you doubt the existence of Witches?"

His smile made her feel like an idiot, but she supposed she had been quite sheltered. Lions stuck close to their Pride. Power in numbers and all that. Plus, her mother was quite hands on.

"I guess I just never thought about them to this extent. I mean, Mom buys all kids of herbs and concoctions from kitchen Witches, but I never thought about the rest of it."

"There is a lot of magic in this world, Ariella. Some of it is right in front of us," he murmured and pulled to a stop in front of a harried looking valet attendant. Brock took her hand in his before she could exit the vehicle.

"Look, I want you to know I am glad you came with me."

"I am too," she responded, knowing he could hear a lie.

It was the truth. Even if she both feared and anticipated the end of the evening with equal parts excitement and anxiety.

Brock walked around the vehicle with the confident gait of a man used to being in charge and tossed his keys to the eager valet. Ariella understood the sentiment all too well. The butterflies in her stomach were doing a mambo as it was.

"Come on."

He took her hand in his big warm one, and those butterflies all seemed to swoon at once. From the second they entered the elegant hotel's entryway, Brock was greeted like an old friend, and she was treated with the utmost respect and courtesy. They surpassed the line and were immediately shown to a snug little booth in the back of the jam packed hotel restaurant.

"How come we didn't have to wait?"

"Oh, well, actually the MC has an interest in this establishment," he said, and she noted his cheeks turn a dusky shade.

Was he embarrassed? She grinned, and he shrugged, trying to play it off. This was a side of him she had never seen. Curiosity got the better of her, so she leaned forward, wanting more from the surprisingly shy, secretive male.

"An interest?"

"Yeah, we have a longstanding friendship with Mr. Stein, and the executive chef as well. In fact, we are expected."

Brock appeared nervous as he sipped his water and looked around, and Ariella wondered why.

"Really? Why would he be expecting us?" she asked, eyebrows raised.

"*She* is always available whenever Brock Laurent drops by," a feminine voice coming from right behind her had Ariella almost falling off the booth.

The woman managed to startle a Lioness. How embarrassing! Ariella swallowed her yowl and took in the tall, thin female. The stranger wore a pristine white chef's coat and a small hat to help hold back the wealth of blond hair that hung in a braid down her back. Her beautiful face was positively perfect.

She was gorgeous, and it seemed she knew Brock. Intimately if her smile was anything to go by. Ariella swallowed the pang of hurt. Why would he take her to meet an old conquest?

"Hello, *mon cher*," she said warmly, and Brock stood up and embraced the stranger with more familiarity than Ariella had been prepared for.

"Susan, you look wonderful," he said, and his smile was genuine as he stepped back to look at her with mischievous blue eyes.

Ariella's stomach dropped. What the hell was this? She looked down, trying to weigh her options, as they continued their familiar greeting ritual.

"As do you, but then you always look well, darling," she touched his face with affection before letting her hand fall back to her side, and once more Ariella's heart twisted.

The woman was clearly in love with him, but Brock seemed to not notice. Was that a thing with him? She wondered unkindly. Did he just collect women's hearts and break them casually without thought or care?

Well, that was it. She had had enough. Before she could stand, Brock's warm hand clamped down on her shoulder and he made small circles with his thumb that immediately soothed her beast.

"I want you to meet someone," Brock said quietly. He looked down at Ariella and his eyes were warm and kind, almost apologetic as he continued. "This is Ariella Golden. Ariella, this is Susan Stoker, the head chef here at *The Cabin*."

"Ah, this is the representative from *Eat Well Live Proud*, the little Lion Pride's corporation you told me about," the woman said.

She was all business now as she sat down with a wide smile. Probably relieved because Brock had placed Ariella in perspective for his lovely friend. Confusion clouded her mind, but Ariella managed to fight through it. She answered Susan's questions with aplomb and courtesy. She was a Lioness after all, majesty was in her blood.

"Brock here has been after me for weeks now to sign over our entire meat and seafood departments to your tiny hands," the chef said and looked Ariella up and down like she was scat.

It was not the first time a female had underestimated Ariella, but she refused to be cowered by the woman. No need for aggression. She was a Lioness, and as such, Ari did not need to announce it.

"Excuse me, ladies. I will leave you to chat while I get us some drinks," Brock murmured.

He stood up and left them alone. Ariella wanted to scream at him for doing so. This was so not the dream date she'd imagined. The skinny blonde eyed her coolly and crossed her legs in the slim black pants she wore under her chef's coat.

"So, what is it that makes you so special that Brock Laurent would not only mention you, but sing your praises and bring you to me in *my* new restaurant?"

"He is a man who knows quality when he sees it," Ariella replied.

She smiled widely, allowing a bit of her inner predator to show through. The moment the woman figured out that she was more than just a harmless female, Ariella felt slightly better. She couldn't put her nose on what Ms. Stoker actually was, but she was not a normal, and not a Shifter either.

"Indeed. So, tell me, are you lovers?"

"I don't see what that has to do with this," Ariella stated. "The fact, Chef Susan, is I work for the finest organically raised meat, fowl, and sustainably harvested seafood distributor in the area. We cater specifically to those businesses frequented and run by people like us. Creatures with a finer palate and heightened appreciation for freshness and quality. Our clients' success is of the utmost importance at *Eat Well Live Proud,* and all of my accounts are handled with care and seen to personally."

"But you deal with small restaurants, yes? Not establishments of this caliber and size."

"I often work with local business, but our corporation is large and internationally known. I more than confident in my ability to meet your needs."

"I see," Susan said and looked up as Brock returned with a bottle of wine in hand. "Ah, 1993 was a wonderful year, wasn't it, Brock?"

Her knowing smile made Ariella cringe internally, but she hid it well as he poured three glasses.

"Ariella is a fan of white wine, aren't you?" he replied and smiled at her in a way that made her heart thump inside her chest.

Bum bum bum.

Her inner Lioness practically swooned at his smile and Ariella grabbed a piece of focaccia from the breadbasket in self-defense. She chewed a bite slowly, trying to calm her nerves. Why did he have such power over her?

With something akin to panic rising inside of her, she swallowed down the lovely dry white wine and winced as it went down the wrong way. Maybe she was just hungry.

"Do you recall the time we hunted for truffles?"

"Of course."

Ariella blocked out their conversation and took another bite of the delicate rosemary infused focaccia. Brock was busy rehashing old times with Chef Susan, and she was entirely out of her depth with their conversation. Talking business was one thing, but with this woman, every word uttered held a memory or innuendo Ariella was not privy to and it was rather annoying.

Ignoring it became something she had to actively work at, and even though the meeting was all of twenty minutes, it felt much, much longer. Ariella had already decided to leave by then, but she would wait for the Chef to go away first, then she would request an Uber.

Finally, and to her utmost delight, a small, dark-haired man wearing a similar chef's coat approached the table and whispered to the woman. Her eyes widened, and she nodded.

"I am sorry to cut this short, but I am needed in the kitchen—"

"No worries, Susan, I understand," Brock said, smiling warmly. He stood up and extended a hand.

Ariella was surprised by his suddenly curt and rushed manner, it seemed he had enjoyed the lady's company, but whatever was going on between them he was happier to see her go. She'd been demanding of his attention and had repeatedly cut Ariella out of their conversation.

But, if she was being fair and diplomatic, Brock had always found a way to bring the topic back to include her. Susan nodded in Ari's direction before addressing the tall, almost too handsome Dire Wolf Shifter once more.

"Well, Brock, it has been too long, and I admit I was surprised when you called me back after weeks of ignoring my messages. But I am angry at you, you didn't tell me it was quite this important."

"I wanted to, Susan, please forgive me," he replied.

"I see, and that is why you did not mention this

creature here. She is quite lovely, your little huntress," Susan said, and Ariella sniffed loudly.

She did not like being spoken about as if she was invisible, but for some reason the predator in her understood something about the woman the human did not. She inhaled again, silently, and found it quite odd that she could not detect a scent other than the herbs and spices that clung to her chef's coat.

"Well, I see no reason to delay. You have convinced me, dear boy. Miss Golden, I would like you to add *The Cabin* to your weekly routes of deliveries as soon as possible. Here is my card," she said and nodded.

The man who had come to fetch her presented Ariella with a plain white card with bold black font that read Susan Stoker, Executive Chef, and had her contact information beneath.

"Oh, yes, of course, I will email you an order form," Ariella said, stunned, but finally recalled how to speak. "You can select what you will require at the end of each week for the following one. We require notice roughly twenty-four hours before you'd like the delivery."

"Perfect. I will look for your email. Ciao, Brock, and goodbye."

"Susan," he nodded.

"*Goodbye*," she reiterated, and winked at Ariella.

If the Lioness inside of her thought the tension had been unbearable when the strange woman had been there, she was in no way prepared for it to worsen after she'd gone. But Ari had given up on playing games.

"What is this all about, Brock? Why did you invite me here?"

"I'm sorry, it must seem odd," he said, exhaling deeply.

"Yes, it is. You have ignored me for a long time. I'm not sophisticated enough to play this way. In fact, I think I should leave. I'm going to call an Uber," Ariella murmured, placing her napkin on the table.

"Wait," he hissed, closing his eyes. Brock reached out and placed it on hers, and she stilled.

Sadness filled her and disappointment. She was confused and her emotions were a wreck. Didn't he know how hard this was for her? Was he using his indecent proposal to make the other woman jealous? What was Chef Susan to him, anyway? So many questions. They battered at her until she thought she would scream her frustration.

"No, Brock, I can't—"

"Please, Ariella, please," he begged, weakening her

defenses. "I promise, I am not playing with you, and it will all make sense, I swear. Just don't go. Stay. Eat with me," he whispered.

Brock nodded his head to someone over her left shoulder, and suddenly a myriad of tasty little plates was set before them. She'd never seen him beg or look so vulnerable. As each dish was placed on the table, he seemed to hold his breath. Like he cared if she liked the selections he'd made.

"I thought you might be hungry by now, so I ordered when I went to get the wine."

Brock motioned towards the dishes, and to her utter embarrassment, Ariella's stomach grumbled. She was starved, but she wasn't a fool. There was something very odd about all this. Something she didn't understand going on behind the scenes with him and with their so-called date turned business meeting.

Give him a chance, her Lioness urged.

Ariella wanted to. She really did. It was incredibly uncharacteristic of her to agree to his indecent proposal, but to have it turn into some kind of farce in her face was almost too much to bear.

"Will you stay?"

His big blue eyes were so clear and dark, like a moonlit pool. There was something about Brock that made her reckless. Something that, if she wasn't very careful, was going to cost her more than her virginity.

Yes, please, her Lioness purred.

Ariella crossed her legs and shook out her napkin before dropping it back on her lap.

"Alright. I'm hungry anyway. Surprise surprise," she added sarcastically.

Ariella huffed out a breath and avoided making eye contact with him. She picked up her fork only to have him take it from her.

"Let me. Here, try this," he whispered and held a tiny little confection with slivers of smoked salmon and caviar to her lips.

She leaned forward, feeling a little silly that he was hand-feeding her in public, but that thought vanished and Ariella moaned aloud the second she nibbled the delectable morsel.

"That is amazing, but it's impossible. The salmon tastes like yours," she said and tilted her head to the side. She couldn't believe her eyes when he seemed to blush.

"I studied under Chef Susan for a time. Many years ago, Ariella," he confessed.

"Oh," she said and wiped her mouth.

"No, love, it was not like that," he explained. "She

has been a friend of the DWMC for many years and was my mother's maid of honor, in fact," he added.

"Wait, I know some Shifters age slowly, but she isn't a Dire Wolf. What is she?" Ariella asked.

"I told you this place was not just Shifter run. Susan is a Vampire and though she may have given the wrong impression, she is more like my aunt. I swear she was never a girlfriend," he said and made a face like the idea would be borderline gross. Ariella laughed aloud, relief filling her.

"I believe you," Ariella said, knowing full well her Lioness would have smelled a lie.

He seemed to relax a bit after that, and they sampled half a dozen more appetizers before a server came out pushing a cart with what looked like an entire rack of lamb.

"*Monsieur?*" the server asked.

"I will carve, thank you," Brock said and stood.

With the utmost concentration, he selected the choicest cuts of rare lamb for Ariella. She bit her lip in amazement. He was catering to her needs, like she was special to him, and the idea was breathtaking.

He filled her plate with expertly roasted meat, adding some of the unique sides and a hint of cucumber mint relish to her plate before he bothered fixing one for himself. Ariella felt cared for in a way no man had ever accomplished. She waited for him to sit before trying the food.

"Don't you like it?" he asked, brow furrowed.

"It is very good," she said and watched as relief and pride seemed to pass across his handsome face.

He really was undeniably good looking. She wondered why he wasn't more like his Pack Mates. Weylin, Phoenix, and Cole all seemed to have a different girl every night. But not Brock. He never dated.

Even before they had met, if Sheila was to be believed, and the woman had no reason to lie. Not that Shifters did to begin with. Too tricky trying to maintain a lie when the people around you could so easily detect it.

"I'm glad you like it," his deep voice had the most delicious rumble, and she turned her attention to him.

"It's wonderful."

"Good. For dessert, I have something else in mind," he said, and his voice held a hint of promise in it that made her knees weak, even though she was already sitting down.

Whatever the Wolf had in mind, Ariella was sure to be game.

Purrrr.

CHAPTER 11

ate. Mate. Mate.

Brock's Dire Wolf had kept up the mantra throughout the entire evening. He couldn't help it. Everything about her, from the surprising way she handled herself with Susan to the way she seemed to accept him on his terms, was remarkable. Perfect even.

After they'd eaten, he took her hand and led her out of the restaurant for the private suite he'd rented for the night. No obligations. No pretenses.

That was what he'd told himself, and now it was his turn to tell her. He could scent her desire and her nervousness. Both were tempting beyond his experience. He could've killed Susan for sitting with them for so long and purposely giving the wrong impression to Ariella.

His honorary aunt, the woman who had taught him almost everything he knew about cooking, was as far from a lover as one could get. No, he hadn't answered her messages because the confounded Vampire would've questioned him about his love life the first chance she had. Furthermore, she would've known immediately that he was hiding something.

As it was, he'd braced himself for a barrage of emails and phone calls he was bound to get after tonight from Susan and his own mother, who had started riding with the Dire Wolf Widows MC after her mate and his father had passed away. Brock wasn't ready for them to get involved just yet.

First, he had to square things with Ariella, and who knew how easy that was going to be given the mixed signals he'd been sending? Fuck and damn, he could've lost her for all his stupidity. That thought alone had his Dire Wolf howling in outrage.

"Wow," Ariella's softly spoken gasp of surprise reached his ears once the suite doors were opened.

Romantic music was playing low in the background, the fire was lit, a table was laid with champagne, and a cart with fresh berries and ingredients for his special zabaglione was set up. Red roses filled every nook and cranny and since they were on the top floor, a skylight above gave them a perfect view of the moon and the stars in the navy velvet sky.

"This is really something," Ariella murmured.

She walked to the far window, her bright gold eyes on the view. Brock was equally ensnared by a vision of beauty, only for him, that vision was her. Hell, he almost swallowed his tongue at the sway of her hips in that killer dress.

Twinkle lights decorated the trees in the court-yard and the lake sparkled with light from the moon. It was a lovely view, and he imagined the hotel would do very well. But he wasn't all that interested in the success of another Stein Luxury Hotel. He was only interested in whether he could make a go of this thing with Ariella. Either way, he owed it to them both to try.

"Brock?"

Ariella turned and startled when she realized he'd stepped right behind her. How could he resist? Her sweet and spicy musk filled his senses, leaving him on edge and needy for just a small taste of the sweet Lioness.

"Yes?"

From this close, he could see the spark of fire in her gold eyes. Fuck, she was so beautiful. Her

Lioness so regal and powerful. He was a lucky Wolf, truly and well beyond what he deserved.

"Why did you bring me here with you? To act as a buffer between you and your family friend?"

"No," he said immediately. "I wanted to finally spend some time with you, Ariella. I know it must be confusing for you."

"Why now? You've been avoiding me like the plague, then you proposition me and idiot that I am I ran at the chance. You must think I'm desperate or foolish, to tell you the truth, I wouldn't even blame you," she said, shrugging and causing the straps of her dress to fall from her smooth shoulders.

"I don't think that at all," he said, voice rough with his beast.

Before she could move to fix the straps of her dress, he replaced the tiny pieces of fabric with his hands. Touching her was like holding a livewire. He couldn't contain his growl as little bites of electric pleasure zapped through him from the mostly platonic contact.

"Fuck, Ari, I have been torturing myself by staying away from you," he growled.

"Why? I don't want you away from me," she moaned, swaying closer and closer until her soft belly came into contact with the hardness he couldn't hide.

Breathing heavily, Brock stilled, waiting for her to react, to move away, but she didn't. She simply rested against him and waited for him to speak.

"Because," he growled in frustration.

"I'm trying to understand, Brock. Help me," she begged.

"I can't be around you and not want to touch you! Fuck, every time I see you, I think about kissing you. I want you, Ariella. My Wolf wants you. Mine," he growled.

His touch on her shoulders grew rough as he pulled her closer. One hand clamped around her neck, the other at the small of her back. She was trembling against him, spiking his protective instincts. Fuck, he wanted her so damn badly. Brock lowered his head slowly, giving her all the time in the world to move back.

That she didn't gave him all the more reason to take what he wanted. And all he wanted was her. Ariella boldly wrapped her arms around his neck, pulling him closer. She lifted her beautiful face to his, opened her lips, and crashed her mouth against Brock's own hard, unrepentant one.

He growled, greedily giving in to the passionate

tempest that seemed to overwhelm him. Their kiss was explosive, complete, and the best fucking thing he had ever experienced in his long life.

"Mine," he growled again, grinding against her mouth and dragging her body against his.

He wanted her with a desperation that almost blinded him to anything else, and yet Brock found himself keenly aware of her at all times. Every whimpering mewl and shaky breath, every wiggle of her body and press of her tongue meant something else.

He read her like a book. Every movement a signal, a clue that he could follow to give her all the pleasure she craved. Everything she wanted and yearned for, he vowed to deliver. That was his sacred vow to her as man, as Wolf, as mate.

"I want you too," she moaned, and it was like music to his ears.

He wanted her alright, but not for one night, as he'd led her to believe. No, Brock wanted her for much more than that. Lifting her in his arms, he carried her to the bed and placed her gently on the silky comforter.

The hotel's design was of the finest quality and expense, which meant muted colors and sublime textures. Everything he looked for in accommodations, which, given he'd spent so much time on the road, might seem unusual, but Brock knew what he liked.

But all the surrounding luxury was nothing compared to the softness of her skin, or the sweet pleasure he took in her kiss. Shrugging off his jacket, he felt her hands tremble as she tugged on his tie and buttons. He wasn't prepared to be quite so gentle, and in one move he tore the fine shirt off his torso and growled aloud as she leaned forward and kissed her way from his navel to his neck.

"Ari, that feels so good. My turn," he growled, and reached for her zipper, noting the way she froze.

"I will stop if you want me to whenever you want me to. All you have to do, Ariella, is just say the word," he said despite his Wolf's warning growl.

"I, I don't want you to stop. It's just, I've never done this. I have never even undressed for a man," she confessed shyly, and her honesty and innocence humbled him.

"I see, maybe we should talk first."

"Oh, I didn't mean for you to stop," she said quickly and bit her lip.

Her cheeks turned pink, and fuck, she was so beautiful. He adored her.

"I plan on giving you everything I have, Ari, but I

have something to tell you," he said as she kissed the corner of his mouth, his lips, and then his chin.

"Brock, please," she said, and ran her short nails over his pecs and abs, stopping just shy of his throbbing cock.

"Don't stop. I'll go mad if you do."

"Ariella," he growled her name,

Her shy touches grew bolder with every swipe and her golden eyes locked onto his. The next time she ran them down his body, she continued down his hips until his shy little virgin mate cupped his balls in one hand and traced him from root to tip with the other.

Brock froze. This was the moment Brock had feared the most. The one when this virginal little hellcat got a glimpse of his size and girth for the first time. Echoes of his past horror came pummeling through his brain, the sounds of the girl who in his youth he'd foolishly believed was meant for him.

"Get away from me with that thing!"

The embarrassment was nothing compared to the deep psychological scars the experience had given him. From that day on he'd never dated a normal, or a virgin, in fact, he never dated at all. He hadn't lived like a monk.

Brock had engaged in sex, but it was infrequent

and mostly with other Shifters who knew the deal. He'd chosen professionals who were well experienced so as not to be afraid of his extraordinary size. Using sex as a means to relieve him of the tension he'd felt every few years or so was all he could do to sate his beast. Those encounters were as impersonal as a handshake, and he never felt good afterwards.

This was something else entirely. No comparison. At all.

"Brock? Where did you go?"

"You, uh, you're touching me," he said as her hands still gently explored him through his pants.

"Yeah, I am," she replied, and grinned shyly. "Is that alright?"

"Yessss."

"Can I see you, too? I want to see you. Take these off," she begged.

"Ariella, I don't want to frighten you," he mumbled and stilled her hand, trying hard not to hate himself at the look of hurt on her face.

"Am I doing something wrong?" she asked.

"No! God, not at all."

"Well, isn't this why you brought me here? A night with you for the roadhouse's business?"

He closed his eyes. Fuck. He knew that had been stupid.

"Actually," he confessed. "That was a ruse to get you here."

The scent of her disappointment crashed into him, and he opened his eyes. Seeing her misery was too much to bear.

"So, you don't want to spend the night with me, and I don't get *Serious Moonlight* as a client?"

"No! I mean, *yes*. Wait—"

"I think you better explain what the hell you're doing, Brock. I mean, you are hot, then cold, then hot again, and I have had about all I can take."

"Okay, look, I brought you here to meet with Susan to get her to sign on with you. This hotel does a huge business, and you'll most likely win your contest and knock your competition out of the park—"

"And is that all you think I care about? I wasn't going to sleep with you because of work, Brock! You're my mate, you idiot! My Lioness knew the second I met you," she yelled and pushed away from him.

The hurt on her face hit him right in the gut. Fuck, he was losing her. He was messing this up. And the hurt was unbearable.

"No. Of course, I didn't think that. Ari, you have to believe me!" Brock scrambled to explain.

"You know what, Brock, this whole thing is a mistake. I was wrong. You can't be my mate."

She struggled to get off the bed in her tight dress, and he used it to his advantage to pin her down beneath him. He couldn't give up now. Not without making her listen.

"Wait, dammit, Ari, I need you to listen. Please," he growled as she struggled beneath him. "I want you so fucking bad right now, if you don't stop squirming Ariella, this is going to go in another direction sooner than either of us is ready for," he growled, and pressed his hips down until she felt the proof of what he was saying.

"Oh!"

"Now, will you listen or not?"

She stilled beneath him. Her chest heaved in her dress as she tried to catch her breath, but he could tell she was still spitting mad. And damn, she was even more beautiful when she was angry.

Shit.

He was a sick fuck. Whatever. The woman was driving him mad.

"I'm fucking this all up, Ari. I have been from the beginning, but maybe I can try to explain."

"You better," she huffed.

"Alright," he eased off of her and they sat face to face while he told her the truth behind his actions.

"I had a girlfriend a long time ago. She was a normal, and we were kids. She was my first kiss. My first date. And I was the first guy she'd ever seen naked. We tried to, *you know*, have sex, but when things got close, she pushed me off and ran away. She was screaming, saying I was killing her because I was *too big* to fit. She said I was not normal, and a girl would have to be crazy to sleep with me," he growled.

Fuck, he hated this. Brock hated having to reveal all his insecurities and past embarrassments, but he owed it to her.

"I am so sorry, Brock, that must've been awful," Ariella whispered and placed her hand on his shoulder.

She met his eyes with nothing but concern in hers. Why should he have been shocked when she was everything kind and sweet and caring in the world? He exhaled the breath he'd been holding in, hope filling him to near bursting.

"Um, are we here just to see if you could have sex with a virgin? To overcome some fear? I know you don't really want me—"

"Not want you? Fuck, I really am an asshole,

aren't I?" Brock groaned and covered his face with his hands. He laughed self-deprecatingly and turned to stand.

"The first time I saw you, I wanted you so damn much. You struck me dumb with your pretty face and gorgeous, guileless eyes. Then, you shocked the shit out of me, climbing on the back of my bike, and wrapping your hands around my waist. I damn near claimed you right there. Your Lioness had it right from the start, Ariella. So did my Dire Wolf. We are fated mates. You belong to me. And I belong to you."

"So you knew? You knew what we are to each other and yet you denied us," she said, and the pain in her voice brought tears to his eyes.

She shook her head and covered her mouth with her hands. The soft gasping noises she made were worse than if she would've balled her hand and punched him in the face. He sure as fuck deserved it. Instead, she sat back on the bed, eyes brimming with tears, the hurt on her face plain as day as she waited for him to continue.

"Finish it," she demanded.

Grrrrr.

His Dire Wolf snarled and snapped, the beast had been angry with him for stopping and talking when he should've been showing her his feelings, and now he was even more angry because he put that sad look on her face. Brock turned and dropped to his knees in front of her. If he was going to confess, he might as well assume the position.

"Ariella," he breathed her name and closed his eyes. "I was a coward. I was scared. I know this might not be enough, but you have haunted my every moment since that very first day. Your golden eyes, that dark curly hair, your incredible body, and that musky scent that invades my senses and completely overpowers me whenever you're near. I want you so much, I don't know what to do. I love you so much. I need you. But I am so afraid I will scare you or hurt you—"

"Wait, that's why you stayed away?" she asked and furrowed her eyebrows. Brock wanted to reach out and smooth the crease, and he did, but she slapped his hand away.

"You're afraid to hurt me," she stated with wonder in her voice.

"Yes. Why do you think I told you that story?"

"I thought you were confessing that you still loved some childhood sweetheart, you jerk!" she yowled and pushed him right off the bed, landing on top of him with a thud.

"Are you alright?" he said, his voice muffled under the fierce hug she was currently giving him.

"Am I alright?" she looked up at him, her eyes wide with wonder, but she didn't appear angry and for that Brock was grateful.

"You said you loved me. I am more than alright, but I want to know one thing."

"What? I'll tell you anything you want to know," he vowed, and meant it.

"Are you going to claim me or what?"

He stilled beneath her. Then, rucking up her dress to her waist so he could move them to a seated position, Brock's hands cupped her ass as he struggled with his Wolf. He didn't know whether to feel relief or like a fucking idiot for wasting so much time.

"I have every intention of claiming you, but first I need to apologize. My ultimate failing and why I am so unworthy of you, is that I knew you were my fated mate, and I still made up this stupid proposition to give you our account for a night with you in the hopes to seduce you into accepting my claim—"

"So, are you saying you don't want to spend the night with me?" she asked, her amber eyes glowing with mischief.

"Of course, I do. But I don't want it as payment.

That's why I brought you here, to *The Cabin*. I'd mentioned *Eat Well Live Proud* a million times and Susan had already agreed to try your products. This account will take you over the top and even though you have Serious Moonlight's business, I don't ever want you to feel obligated to be with me because of that."

"Brock, you are the dumbest Wolf in the world. Now, shut up and kiss me," she growled and leaned forward, crashing her mouth to his.

He couldn't believe it. She was kissing him. Even after every stupid idiot move he'd made. That was probably why he wasn't prepared when she shoved on his chest and pushing them back onto the carpeted floor with a heavy thud.

"You ambulance chasing jerk!"

His arms were still full of his sassy Lioness, but this time she was cursing and wailing on him. The next punch she threw was caught gently with his fist.

"What? What's wrong? I told you everything—"

"That is what's wrong. You bone-burying, hydrant-pissing, butt-sniffing furball! You've told me everything. All these months, you made me think you didn't want me, that you found me lacking, and here you are telling me everything and I, I just don't know what to say to you," she growled and sat up, still straddling his hips. Her tight dress was still bunched around her waist, revealing long, smooth legs, and sexy lace panties he wanted to rip off with his teeth. His beast surged forward once more.

"I know. You're right, Ariella, let me make it up to you? Let me show you how much I want you. I will do whatever you say. You are in control here. I'm yours, Ari. All yours. If you still want me."

His heart pounded like a steel drum inside of his chest, and he could hardly breathe waiting for her answer. He needed this chance, this opportunity to show her what they could have, what it would mean to be mated to him. Brock had waited almost too long time to stake his claim. He'd fucked up, he freely admitted that. But the heat in her golden gaze told him he still had a chance. He just couldn't fuck it up again.

"How do I know you won't hurt me again?"

"Because it would be like hurting myself. My Wolf would gut me if I even tried. Even I'm not that dumb. Now, come here, hellcat, let me have you," he growled.

Mine.

CHAPTER 12

Ariella didn't know whether to scream or cry after Brock finished his confession. Mostly, she felt confused. The big, gorgeous dummy was scared from some teenage incident she'd rather not think about, and that was why he'd been avoiding her.

"So, when I announced my virginity the other night. It probably didn't help with your insecurities, huh?" she asked, and worried her lower lip.

"Actually, that might've pushed my Dire Wolf over the edge. My animal is chomping at the bit, dying to claim you before anyone else gets any ideas. Knowing I will be your only lover is driving him insane."

"I see. Possessive much?" she asked as he slowly

sat up with her, his hands caressing her bare hips.

Dang it.

She hadn't noticed their positions until now. Her dress was up around her waist, revealing more of her than she'd have liked. Heat flamed her face, but before she could wiggle away, Brock was there kissing her shoulder, then her neck, her cheeks next, and her mouth last.

The slow invasion of his tongue was seductive and hypnotic, rousing as all hell, too. She was quite aware of what was happening, but in that precise moment she would've done anything he wanted. Striptease, rip her clothes off, parade around stark naked, as long as he didn't stop kissing her.

"I want you on the bed," he whispered, and she felt herself nodding.

Before she could slide off him, her powerful mate was already lifting her up from their position on the carpet. He stood with her in his arms as if she weighed nothing at all, and crazy as it seemed, she felt cherished and cared for in that position.

The scent of his Dire Wolf beneath his skin was making her Lioness go crazy. So, hell yes, Ariella thought the bed sounded like a great idea. What better place to get him naked? Then she could rub herself all over his body, mark him with her scent, then stake her claim with her fangs and claws, too.

Rawrrr.

Her pulse raced as she recognized the signs of mating fever taking hold. Whatever Brock was afraid of happening between them, he probably hadn't considered the fact she was an apex predator herself and more than capable of handling anything he could dish out.

The question was, could he handle her?

So far, so good.

"I got you. This okay?" he asked permission even as he gently sat her down on the bed and unzipped her dress.

Ariella couldn't nod her head fast enough. Her skin was boiling. She needed the dress off now. Moisture pooled in her panties, readying her body for his invasion. Seeing him in his pants made her feel seriously anxious and impatient. Her mate had too many clothes on.

"Not yet," he growled and smirked as he caught her staring. Her own growl reverberated in her throat.

"Don't worry, my little hellcat, I promise you will have as much of me as you want. No more, no less."

She believed him, and yet somehow, she knew he

was going to take some convincing. Ariella wanted all of him. Every last inch.

He was her fated mate. Ari was built just for him, and she was going to stake her claim and lay to rest every one of his fears. Tonight, they would begin their lives together.

"I want it all, Brock," she whispered, purring her contentment as he petted her skin, removing her dress.

Brock leaned back on his heels, a deep rumble reverberated in his chest as he stared at her body in the tiny lace panties she had on. The dress had a built-in bra, making it possible for her to wear anything else beneath the silky, hip hugging fabric. She felt empowered and beautiful under his stare.

Going up on her knees, she leaned down, facing him on all fours. Her large breasts swayed, and her sex grew even wetter, desire building inside until she was panting with it. She crawled forward until her face was right in front of that part of him she wanted most. What a shame he'd kept his beautiful cock under lock and key because of some bad memory.

"Ariella," he growled her name.

Brock ran his big hands over her shoulders, down her back to the curve of her ass, tracing the little heart tattoo she'd gotten just over her right cheek when she'd been in college.

"Who put this there?" he grumbled the question.

"Toni," she answered and grinned at his snarled response before she added, "my sister."

"Naughty hellcat," he grunted and pinched her on that same cheek.

Her nipples pebbled under his rapt attention and moisture dripped down her thighs, but she was too curious to give up her position on her knees. Hands reached for his waistband, and his growl grew louder.

"Brock, let me see you," she begged.

"Ari," he grunted, but she was already unzipping the exquisite black fabric and sliding it down his muscular thighs.

He stood still as she undressed him, allowing her to explore with her eyes and hands. Beneath his pants he wore tight black navy blue briefs, and as lovely as they were, Ari knew they had to go. Looking up at him, she raised one finger on her right hand, and popping a single sharp claw, she cocked her head to the side and waited.

"I'm all yours, hellcat. But, uh, be careful with that thing," he tried to joke, but she knew he was tense.

Not for long, her Lioness promised.

She was eager for him. The wild forest scent that clung to him was doing all kinds of marvelous things to her insides, spurring her on, making her wild with desire. She couldn't wait until her skin was covered in his scent, marked with his bite, and filled with his delicious sex.

"Mine," she growled and sliced through the fabric.

"Oh, wow, s'beautiful," she hissed.

His scent was stronger now. He smelled like mature pine trees and clean earth to her sensitive nose. She couldn't wait for a taste.

Prrrrr.

She inhaled and this time his scent was pure and strong like his Wolf after a good hard run. Then it was like promises and laughter. And pure, hot sex. Ariella was running on instinct now, and she couldn't seem to help herself. Brock licked his lips and watched her, his blue eyes glowing with curiosity and his Dire Wolf.

She reached up and kissed his face, tangling her tongue with his until he was moaning and growling into her mouth. He was so fucking hot, and all her thoughts were on him. Brock was her mate, her one and only, and she wanted him to know just how she felt about that fact.

It was time.

Ariella kissed his lips one last time, licking and nibbling her way down his neck and chest. She swirled her tongue around each flat male nipple and loving the hiss that escaped his mouth as she took one between her teeth and gave it a good tug.

"Ari," he moaned her name, and she felt him swell against her belly as she made her way down to that part of him, she so desperately wanted.

His hard abs contracted as she leaned forward and stroked his thick, long cock with her hand. Fuck, he really was so big and thick. She needed both hands to wrap around all of him. She had seen naked men before.

Duh.

Ariella was a Lioness. Nudity was part and parcel of the whole Shifter gig. But she had never seen anything quite as superb as her mate, naked and fully aroused. Brock's legs were thick and heavily muscled, much like the rest of his six-foot five-inch frame. His dark blond hair hung down over his forehead and his blue eyes glowed as he focused on her every move. But she wasn't quite done looking just yet.

He had a smattering of darker blond hair on his chest and upper thighs. And a nest of soft curls that crowned his gloriously thick dick. She leaned down, pressing her face close to him, and felt him throb involuntarily.

Ariella couldn't have stopped herself even if she wanted to. She opened her plump lips, watching him from underneath her thick eyelashes, and licked her way from root to tip, swallowing down the pearl-sized drop of precum that seemed to swell at the slit just for her.

He growled loudly, nostrils flaring and fists at his sides as she swiped him once, twice more with the flat of her tongue. Damn, he tasted delicious. His cock was gorgeous, magnificently formed with a perfect mushroomed head and a thick, even girth from stem to tip. He had a slight curve that was making her legs tremble in anticipation.

This was a perfect cock.

And though she was a virgin, this was something she and her sisters had discussed at length during one of their many slumber parties. Ariella had hit the jackpot, *er,* make that the *cockpot!* She couldn't wait for him to fill her.

"Brock," she moaned as she bent down to continue her new favorite pastime.

Loving on her man with the flat of her tongue. He was incredible and she wanted to show him just how much she appreciated his size. Silly man, thinking he could scare her with what she was guessing was thirteen and a half inches of rock hard gorgeousness.

"Fuck, Ari, I'm gonna come if you don't stop," he growled with his hands fisted at his sides.

"I want you to come," she growled back, taking hold of him with one hand. Ariella pumped his shaft even as she swallowed down as much of him as she could.

Even the ridiculous dildos her sisters had stuffed inside her gift basket couldn't have prepared her for the sheer size and raw beauty of Brock's incredible sex. He was so thick and hard, but his skin was soft like velvet, and he tasted incredible. She just couldn't stop sucking on him.

She swirled her tongue up and down around his wide girth, and soon he was moving with her, flexing his hips, and gripping her head with his hands. Good, she wasn't a delicate flower. Ariella was a powerful Lioness, a strong as fuck she-Cat and a hunter in her own right. She could and would give her mate pleasure.

"Fuck, Ari," he growled louder, and she moved faster.

Licking, sucking, and pumping, finally, Ariella lifted her mouth and pressed his cock between her large breasts. Her own pussy throbbed in need, but this was about him, about his learning that she could take him any which way, and what was more, she wanted to.

Brock growled aloud as his orgasm rushed over him, and her Lioness echoed the sound. Her inner feline loved the way his hot cum felt across her chest, marking her in his scent and claiming her in this small way was the best fucking feeling in the world.

It was raw and primal, but in the best possible sense. Her mate had finally marked her, and she hoped it was the first of many times to come for them both. Brock's chest still reverberated with his growl, and his nostrils flared as his eyes zeroed in on Ariella's breasts.

"Let me clean you, hellcat," his voice was gravelly as he moved.

Moving quickly to the bathroom, he returned with a wet washcloth and gently wiped her clean with it. What had started as perfunctory soon became seductive, and she could hardly keep quiet as he smoothed his skillful hands over her pebbled nipples. Brock pressed her breasts together, adding his tongue to the mix as he suckled her until she was writhing beneath him.

"You're so beautiful," he growled, coveting her with his body.

"Mine. Tell me you're mine, Ariella," he groaned, and she loved the possessive edge to his voice.

"I am yours," she answered.

Of course she was. Always had been, and wasn't that the truth?

"There's no going back now. You are it for me, Ari. I love you," he declared, and his eyes met hers before his lips crashed against hers.

Ariella wrapped her legs around his waist, bringing him into stark contact with her needy sex. This was everything and the only thing she had wanted since meeting him. The physical expression of her commitment, her feeling for him, was vital to her very being. Shifters ran on instinct, and there was nothing more natural than wanting to be claimed by her mate.

"I only want to move forward, Brock. With you. Only you."

"Good mate," he growled. "Now it's my turn," Brock hissed as he slid down her body.

Her Lioness wanted to snarl and order him to come back. She wanted to feel more of that wonderful cock of his pressing deep, so deep inside, she'd be blind to everything but it. But it seemed her soon-to-be mate had other ideas.

"You're not the only one who likes to lick, my sassy little hellcat," he said gruffly, as if he'd heard her beast's whine, and maybe he had.

Fated mates could sometimes get inklings of each other's feelings even before the matebond was fully formed. It only spoke of how perfect they were for each other. And Brock was perfect for her. And he proved it by driving her out of her mind.

Brock's sexy growl vibrated through her body as he dropped hot, biting kisses down her body. She moaned aloud as his hot breath came into contact with her throbbing sex. Then she couldn't think anymore.

He pressed his nose against her soaked folds and inhaled a deep breath. He sucked in a deep breath, seeming to savor the scent of her heat if his growl was anything to go by. Tiny little electrical currents rocketed through her body, turning into lightning bolts as the pressure of Brock's tongue increased. He swiped a path from her asshole to her clit in a move so singularly perfect she almost came right then and there.

Her body tensed and the Lioness inside of her purred loudly as he pressed her knees farther apart with his hands, granting him better access. Brock's growling reverberated from his mouth through her core, the rapt attention making her more and more susceptible to every nuance of that fine-tuned appendage.

"Brock," she moaned his name, and pulled on his hair.

"That's it, my little hellcat. Sexy little purr, sweeter than my Harley. Gimme more," he growled and slid a finger into her slick heat as his tongue flicked back and forth over her swollen clit.

Fuck yeah. She purred. Louder. Stronger. Harder, so hard. She damn near fell off the bed from the vibrations alone.

"Close," she growled, and tugged tighter on his thick hair until he was right where she wanted him.

"Come for me, Ari," he commanded, and his tongue and finger worked in time to push her right over the edge.

There it was. So close. Right in front of her. She could almost taste it. Harder. Faster. Bliss waited at the end of the road. All she had to do was grab it.

And suddenly, Ari bucked her hips, grinding her pussy into Brock's mouth until it was right there.

There, there, there, oh fuck! RIGHT THERE!

Ariella roared as her first ever orgasm with a man raced through her. She hardly noticed Brock slide up her body until he was pressing his thick cock slowly and surely inside of her tight, slick sheath. Pressure filled her, stretching, burning so damn good.

Fuck.

She had no experience with anything like this, and while his mere size was shockingly bigger than expected, everything about him was perfect. He was beyond anything she could've ever imagined. And in the best possible way. She felt him everywhere. Aftershocks of her first orgasm kept zipping through her with every slip and grind of his thick sex. Her mate truly was fantastic.

"You okay? Am I hurting you?" he asked, concern shining in his Wolfishly blue eyes.

"S'perfect, Brock. So good."

She meant that. Literally. Everything about him was good. And together, they were perfect. Brock leaned down, nuzzling her mouth, kissing her deeply, and driving her mad. He held himself still, giving her time to adjust, but Ariella didn't want that kind of treatment. She nipped his lip and almost laughed when he pulled his head back in shock.

"What was that for?"

"That was just a taste of what's gonna happen to you if you don't stop fucking around, Brock Laurent. Claim. Me. Now," she growled and watched as his eyes went from confused to focused.

"Hellcat," he growled.

"Damn straight."

"Mine," he replied and pulled out inch by delicious inch, only to slam back in all the way to the hilt.

"Yes. And you are mine," she growled, tugging him closer and mashing her mouth to his.

Mine. Mine. MINE. RAWRRRR!

CHAPTER 13

*M*ine. *All mine. My Ariella. Mate.*

His Wolf could not stop celebrating the fact his mate was well and truly claimed. Their first time together had been incredible. Life altering. And Brock was still reeling from it.

He separated half a dozen eggs and grabbed the large wire whisk, keeping the flame on the copper pot low as he prepared Ariella's favorite dessert. He'd gleaned that little tidbit after a brief conversation with her mother, who'd called him up to tear him a new asshole the night he'd propositioned her daughter.

His opinion of Patricia Golden had changed dramatically after that conversation. His little hellcat had a lot of her mother's spunk, and he admired the clever way Patty had described, in detail, what she was going to do to him if he did not change his ways. He'd promised her he meant only the best for her daughter, and afterward, the Lioness was thrilled.

"My girl always wanted a puppy. Be sure to behave or I'll have you fixed," were her exact words.

The imagery still made him shake his head. Patty, as she insisted he call her, was certifiable in some ways. Damn entertaining in others.

Of course, Ariella hadn't been aware of that little conversation before they'd spent the last couple of hours claiming each other all over the luxury suite he'd rented. They had no secrets between them now. Like none.

Brock had never felt happier. There were no words to describe the heaven he experienced sliding into her sweet body and knowing he was the only one who would ever get to have her. She was his now. And he was hers. In every sense of the word.

Brock Laurent and Ariella Golden were well and truly mated.

Fuck, just thinking about it made him grin like an idiot, but he didn't care. He'd never felt better. Her body was a wonderland made just for him. Every supple curve and valley, a place for him to worship and explore. He'd memorized every nuance as best he could by sight, touch, scent, and taste, and he looked forward to experiencing every change the future had in store for the both of them.

She was sublime. Designed by the fates as if specifically ordered. She suited every one of his preferences, and gods be blessed, he filled hers. Her spicy musk scent was ecstasy inducing, and now it was ingrained inside of him.

He lived for her responsiveness. Fuck, her sighs, moans, shivers, and shakes drove him insane. The feel of her pussy rippling around his cock as he'd brought her to orgasm again and again, got better each and every time they made love. Brock was one lucky sonovabitch. Ariella had taken to his size and appetite with gusto.

He worried at first, because he was insatiable. Brock wanted her again, right now, and it had only been a few minutes since they'd last made love. Yes, it was love. He loved her. Everything about her. She was multi-faceted, shy, and sweet even with her sailor potty mouth, Maybe even because of it.

She was cute as hell when she was pissed. Aggressive as she was disarming, brilliant and confident, while at the same time humble and unassuming. Fuck, he loved every inch of her, inside and out.

"Favorite color?" she asked from her place on the bed while he got the food ready.

They'd been playing twenty questions on and off for hours, and while they knew most things about each other, he liked the game.

"Amber," he said, and she laughed at him. Her eyes were stunning and were the exact shade he preferred.

"Mine's blue," she returned pertly.

"Favorite book?" he asked.

"Hmm. I have to think about that. I am a whore for indie romance books," she said, and while she pondered titles, he whisked.

Mated Dire Wolves were said to become so enamored of their mates that they became the sole purpose of their existence. He'd been troubled by that description in his youth, but he was just fucking fine with that now. No more doubts or misgivings. The sassy little hellcat was all his. Belonging to her in return was his new favorite thing.

Brock would spend every moment of his life making sure Ariella knew just how wholly and completely she was wanted and loved by him. They'd both professed their feelings a dozen times over the night, and being Shifters, they knew they spoke the truth about it. The strength of their love was evident in their matebond. Powerful and strong, even now he could feel it pulsing softly around them.

"Mmm, that smells divine," Ariella moaned.

Damn, he loved her vocalizations. She rolled over onto her side, and he got a view that was so fucking amazing he almost burned the sugar. Brock grunted and refocused, whipping the delicate Italian cream dessert into little fluffy peaks in no time.

He scooped it into the little ceramic bowls the staff had left them and added slices of strawberries and plump raspberries. Grinning, he walked over to the bed with the fragrant confection in his hands.

"Is that for me?" she asked, biting her lip, and wagging her eyebrows.

Ari sat up, reaching for the bowl, but Brock shook his head. He pushed her gently back onto a mound of pillows behind her.

"Sort of. See, this one is for you," he growled and fed her a raspberry.

"Mmm."

"And this part is for me," he grunted, lifting a slice of strawberry dripping zabaglione.

Ari gasped as he dropped the warm cream and

fruit onto one of her own little ripe berries. The confection landed perfectly on one pert nipple, and he did the same to the other. She giggled. The sound soon turned into a long, drawn out moan, as he licked the sweet dessert off, suckling her breasts until they were clean.

"I'm still hungry," he grumbled, and she gasped again as he added another dollop to her navel.

"Are you going to share?" she asked, but he held the bowl just out of reach.

"Maybe, but only if you moan like you did the last time you were at *Serious Moonlight* eating the dish I made for your brother," he grinned and held a plump raspberry dipped in cream between his lips.

"You heard that, did you?"

Brock nodded and wagged his eyebrows. Ariella leaned forward and claimed her prize, chewing the berry with a deep, throaty moan that went straight to his cock before claiming his lips once more.

"I love the noises you make when you eat," he growled and licked cream from her inner thigh.

"You do, huh?"

"Uh huh."

Brock focused his attentions to her luscious curves. Bite for bite, he fed her dessert from interesting body parts until they were both a sticky, sweaty mess.

"Time for a bath," he growled and lifted her up like the cherished treasure she was.

He carried her to the large bathroom where he'd already started filling the enormous tub with warm water.

"Brock?"

"What is it, hellcat? Do you need something?"

"Yes," she said, pulling his head down for one of her soul-searing kisses. "You. I need you."

That soft plea was Brock's undoing as he followed her into the tub. Sitting with his legs straight out on the bottom, he lifted her over him, loving the way she thrust her chest out and opened her legs, sliding down and taking his thick cock inside of her with one sublime roll of her hips.

"Fuck, Ari, you bring me to my knees. Do you know that?"

"Good," she moaned and rocked again.

That was just like her, he thought, and squeezed the perfectly round globes of her ass, lifting her higher and slamming her back down as hard as the water allowed. She fit him perfectly. Like a vise, gripping and caressing his cock with every subtle flex and roll.

Strong. Supple, Sumptuous female.

Much to his delight, she appeared just as enamored of him as he was with her. Her appetite matched his, and fuck, he had to admit he liked every little thing she did.

His Wolf howled inside of him, the beast so fucking elated after finally having claimed his mate. In fact, claiming her again was a top priority at the moment. He just had to wait for that moment when her sweet pussy would clench and ripple with the start of orgasm.

So, why not help it along? His sly Wolf growled, and Brock liked the suggestion.

He claimed her mouth with his, kissing her deeply, thrusting his tongue in and out of her mouth, mimicking the invasion of his dick inside her hot channel. He increased speed and strength, taking control by lifting her and bringing her back down, faster, harder until her walls began to contract, and she dropped her head back.

Then he struck, his canines sliced through her skin just above her breast and he swallowed down her life's force even as her sex squeezed and milked him. Pleasure like he'd never experienced built up inside of him as her sharp Lioness' claws raked the skin of his shoulders.

She had already bitten him, but he'd heard tales of Big Cats who twice-marked their mates. Feeling it, of course, was something else entirely. His shoulders were on fire, but that paled compared to the raw pleasure that was coursing through his veins.

"Love you, mate," Ariella whispered as she clung to him in the aftermaths of their shared orgasm.

He felt her love wrap around him, pulsing through their matebond, and wanted to howl it to the entire world. Ariella loved him, and Brock was the luckiest fucker on the planet.

After a good long nap, he ordered them both some clothes from the boutique in the hotel lobby. With breakfast finished and another shower behind them, Brock and Ariella headed back to her condo in Blue Valley. It was, after all, a workday, and although she'd be a tad bit late, it was important she went in.

"I could call out," she said, but he shook his head.

"Nope. Come on, get your things. Today is the day, and you worked too hard to miss it. I'll wait for you, love," he encouraged, smiling at her like she hung the moon.

"Okay, I'll just be a minute," she said and stepped over the remnants of chips, salsa, and tequila.

He quirked his eyebrow before shrugging. Brock knew her sisters and mother had been there last night. The females must've continued with their little party, and of course, they hadn't bothered cleaning up. He shook his head as he cleared away the debris and started the dishwasher.

"What are you doing here?"

Patricia Golden came tumbling out of one of the closed bedroom doors, wearing a large silk caftan with her hair sticking up in all directions. He cleared his throat and poured his mate's mother a mug of the coffee he'd just brewed.

"Good morning, Patty. Ariella is just changing for work, and I thought I would clean up a bit for her," he said.

"Shhh! Do you have to be so loud?"

"Oh—" Brock tried not to laugh, but it was difficult. "I apologize, ma'am."

"Don't you ma'am me," she sniffed and drank deeply from her mug. "So, did you claim her yet?"

"Uh, yes, Ariella and I are mated," he smiled as he said it, but when the woman didn't respond, he looked up to find her squinting at him, arms crossed defensively over her chest.

"*Hmph.* Well, you better do right by her, or I swear to the gods you'll find yourself neutered and tagged for the pound, you hear me?"

"Uh, yes, of course, I would never hurt her in any way."

"I don't want to hear it. You just give her space and let her be herself. Mating isn't about taking over someone's life, you know," she mumbled, but stopped as Ariella strolled back in.

She was wearing a dark brown pencil skirt and a buff colored silk blouse that was almost sheer. His mouth went dry. Damn, she was beautiful, but she looked nervous.

"Hey," he said and walked up to her, handing her the cup of coffee. "Did you email Susan, yet?"

"Yes, last night when you said, but Brock—"

"Drink this," he instructed and rubbed her shoulders while she took a hearty sip of the coffee he'd prepared just the way she liked it—strong with a drop of cream and one sugar.

His Wolf liked the idea of providing for her, of giving her sustenance from now until eternity. Of course, he wanted to hunt and drop dead animals on her doorstep, but for now, he figured this was better.

"You are walking in there today with both *The Cabin* and *Serious Moonlight* under your belt," he began. "You are going to knock them dead, my little hellcat."

"After the whole basket incident, I don't know if I could take another day of pranks and Cornelia's snootiness," she mumbled.

"What basket?" he asked curiously.

Grrrrr.

CHAPTER 14

"What basket?"

Shit.

Had she said that out loud? Ariella groaned at her faux pas having neglected mentioning the dildo basket and chew toys, for obvious reasons.

"Show him, honey!" Patricia laughed from her perch on one of the stools surrounding the kitchen counter, and Ariella's eyes landed on her nosy matriarch.

How had she missed the fact her own mother was sitting there listening to them?

"Mom," she moaned and closed her eyes.

Just then Brock leaned over and nuzzled her neck, the little gesture of affection did more for her than any number of cups of coffee. And the fact he did it in front of her mother?

Sigh. Huge bonus points for her little Pookie.

She'd dubbed him that after a bout of tickling last night where she'd tried to make him heel using the names Fido and Spot. Of course, by the time she'd gotten to Pookie, she had his balls in her hand, literally, and smart man that he was, he gave in. The nickname was going to stick, but only in the bedroom she'd promised.

Public displays of affection only meant one thing in the Shifter world, he was seriously in love with his mate. It was one thing to bring a girl to orgasm dozens of times behind the closed doors of a hotel suite where no one could hear or see them, and quite another to drop a tender kiss on her neck in front of her mom.

While she thoroughly enjoyed the hotel escapades, Ariella admitted to being a little nervous about how he would react back on their home turf. As it was, this was her place, not his. The jury was still out on that one, but she had to give him credit. Brock had been nothing but supportive and encouraging all morning.

"What? It's over there," Patricia said and pointed —unhelpfully—in the direction of the horrible thing.

"Mom, *ixnay* on the *asketbay*!" Ariella hissed at the woman.

"I admit, I'm curious."

Brock smirked and walked over to where her mother and sisters had been hanging out the night before, obviously pawing through their gag gift. She closed her eyes as Brock sifted through the goods, listening for the slam of the door as he walked out on her, but surprisingly, it didn't come.

In fact, her amazing Dire Wolf mate just chuckled out loud. She blinked up to see him holding the gallon of lube in one hand and the elephant-simulated-cock dildo in the other.

"Is this supposed to be for you or me? Never mind, I don't want to know," he mumbled and shook his head.

"It was a stupid gag because of the night *mommy dearest* dosed me. You know, when I announced I was a virgin in the bar," she whispered, knowing full well her mother could hear her perfectly.

"I see," he said and dropped the small-compared-to-his—*lucky her*—elephant cock dildo and picked up the bag of peanut butter puppy treats.

"And who is this for?"

"Oh, dang it," she moaned and covered her face with her hands.

Ariella ignored his deep chuckle as he walked back over to her. She felt his large hands cover her hips as he pulled her up against his big, tall body and wrapped her up in his steely arms. She loved being close to him, loved how he made her feel small, despite being a curvy woman.

"Uncover your eyes, Ariella. Come on, you can tell me," his tone soothed her frayed nerves, and she knew it was his Dire Wolf reaching out to the Lioness through their matebond. Still, she did as he asked.

"I knew you were my mate the first time I met you, and I kinda sorta confided in my sisters," she said.

"And they thought puppy treats and chew toys would win me over, huh?"

He furrowed his dark blond brows and Ariella bit her lip.

Shit.

He was gonna think they were freaks! This was it. The moment he walked out on her. Ariella huffed an exasperated breath. If he couldn't take a joke, he could just keep on walking. Her sisters were natural pranksters and if he was her true mate, he would just have to deal with it. But inside, she was shaking like a leaf on a tree.

"Wait till they get their Christmas presents," he promised and bit her gently on her ear.

"You really are perfect," she moaned and squeezed him to her.

"Enough with the PDAs. I'm your mom, and this is gross."

Brock laughed, and Ariella sighed in relief. Her mom was a lot, but she was still her mother. She loved that he could just take it all in with a chuckle and a hug.

Ariella felt like laughing and crying and yelling all at the same time. Her hormones were completely out of control. She wanted to rub herself all over him *again*, and yet, she wanted to yowl at him for making her nuts.

"Hey, you better leave, your sister just texted me. The quarterly meeting is starting early. Apparently, Corny has some announcement," her mother interrupted and Ari was back to wanting to scream in frustration.

"Come on, my car is faster," Brock winked.

He was right. In no time at all, he was pulling up to her office building. She grabbed the handle of the car door and looked at him. Reluctant to leave him so soon after their mating, she leaned over and kissed him quickly. There was so much still unsaid, but she needed to get in there.

"I'll come get you when you're finished, yes?"

"Yes," she smiled nervously.

"Ariella, I love you. We're mated now, and it's all gonna be okay. Now, go show them what you're made of, my little hellcat."

She nodded again and hurried to the door. The office was dead quiet, which was not all that odd, since everyone was inside the conference room. Ms. Pierce was sitting and listening to Cornelia, who had the floor, when Ariella slipped inside.

"It has come to my attention that one of our own has been using her body to get clients! Bargaining sex for a leg up to win this quarterly competition. I have a folder here with images of the person in question, and I think, Ms. Pierce, that you will want to act accordingly," Cornelia said, grinning triumphantly as she walked forward.

"Oh my!" Maggie Pierce's eyes bulged out of her head as she quickly peeked inside the envelope.

Whispers ran rampant around the room. Mainly because no one could figure out how Cornelia had the balls to out someone else for using sex as a trading tool for work. It was well-known she slept around with her clients to secure their accounts. The cheap cheating hussy!

"I am telling the truth about Ariella Golden," Cornelia said loudly and nodded at Ariella, who up until that time did not know what was going on.

"Wait? What?" Ari gasped, eyes wide.

"I have pictures of you naked with one of your clients and we can only imagine what you were doing to get that account," she said haughtily, and Ariella wondered if the she-Cat believed her own bullshit.

"Well, I admit I am truly shocked, Ms. Golden, you see, before you finished updating your portfolio this morning, you were behind Cornelia here in the quarterly contest—"

"Yes, and it isn't fair. She shouldn't win with *Serious Moonlight's* account after banging the head chef to get it! Admit it. You're not a virgin anymore, you had sex with that dog!" Cornelia screeched.

Ariella was shaking in her shoes, but not with fear. It was rage. Pure and unfiltered, and she was doing her best not to let her she-Cat out, but hearing that woman speak ill of her mate was so not a good thing.

"Ariella? Are you in a relationship with Chef Laurent?" Maggie asked.

There was no way around it. She had to answer, but this was wholly unfair. Stilling herself against the fury of her inner feline, Ariella took a steadying breath before she answered.

"He is my mate."

"You see! Mates can't stay away from each other. I bet she still reeks of his scent, don't you? Imagine coming in here smelling like dog—"

"Cornelia, one more word out of you," Ariella threatened, but Ms. Pierce held up a hand to silence the women.

"And yet, Cornelia," Ms. Pierce continued. "Ms. Golden hasn't updated the Dire Wolves' account, have you Ariella?"

"No, I haven't," she smirked and listened to the gasps from everyone in the room.

It was common knowledge she'd been after that account for months. But unbeknownst to all but her, she'd already switched the account to her sister Antonette's profile. Ever grateful for the support of her siblings, she felt their combined strength as they stood behind her.

The Golden girls indeed.

She smirked at a baffled-looking Cornelia. The Goldens were known for being pranksters, but they always had each other's backs. Unnecessary as it was, since no one really liked Cornelia, and this latest display was more than the pot calling the kettle black. It was indescribably juvenile and petty.

"But she's been lusting after their head chef for months now and this proves he only gave her the account after she performed sexual favors on that stuck up, conceited Wolf," Cornelia grumbled and stomped her foot as she spoke.

"What did you call my mate?" she hissed, her inner she-Cat had been pacing ever since she'd heard the woman talk about her Pookie.

"This isn't fair!" Cornelia gasped as Ariella leaped over the table and had the woman by the throat.

"My mate is none of your business," Ariella growled into Cornelia's suddenly very pale face.

So, her Lioness was a little territorial. Could you blame her? Her mating mark was barely scarred over, and this chick was challenging her position as a mated feline.

Hell. No.

The whispers in the room grew louder after that and it was all Ariella could do to control her beast and stop her from snapping the woman's neck like a twig.

"Oh snap."

"Damn."

"Corny is about to get her ass whupped."

"Ariella," Ms. Pierce interrupted. "That is enough, I think."

Ariella let go of Cornelia and blinked down at her boss. After all her hard work, was she really going to lose this quarter because of this? She was about to speak when Ms. Pierce held up her hand.

"Cornelia, head over to HR and sign up for our classes on sexual harassment and bullying, or else pack up your desk and get gone," Mrs. Pierce commanded.

She waited as the other woman hurriedly grabbed her belongings and headed out the door.

"As for everyone here, I suppose it's only fair that I announce the winner of this month's quarterly contest. By landing the most small business accounts in this state, and the next two to the north of us, and securing a brand new major hotel, which is part of a much larger chain and has enormous potential for growth, Ariella Golden, you have won yourself a paid vacation for two to *Moongate Island*! I suggest you bring your new mate," Ms. Pierce announced and smiled as she extended a hand for Ariella to shake.

The room broke out into applause, and congratulations were shouted. Ariella could hardly believe it.

Then again, she had totally worked her butt off and Cornelia was really just a big jerk. Whatever that woman's malfunction, Ari hoped she figured it out—albeit very far away from Ariella and her mate.

She laughed and smiled with everyone as they sliced cakes and passed around other munchies, as Lion Shifters were wont to do. After she had outlined the details of her new client, *The Cabin*, and secured their upcoming order courtesy of Chef Susan—which was admittedly bigger than any of her other clients—Ariella sat back down and listened as the others gave their own reports with barely concealed impatience. The urgency to leave to be with her mate was growing with every passing minute.

Her Lioness was pacing in the metaphysical plane where the creature waited till called. The large feline rubbing against her skin. She wanted out. She wanted her mate. The minutes ticked by, and Ariella did her best to soothe the animal. Not an easy feat with a kitty who was actively experiencing mate withdrawal.

"These are for you," Ms. Pierce said and handed Ariella the manilla envelope Cornelia had given her and whispered in her ear. "You go on and get out of here, Ms. Golden. Start your vacation right now. You deserve it. Oh, and Ariella? My congratulations on your *very impressive* mate."

The older woman winked, and Ariella blushed furiously. Whatever was inside that envelope would have to wait. She wasn't opening it with her snooping sisters peeking over her shoulder.

Her thoughts traveled back to Brock, and she felt her whole body glow. She couldn't wait to see him. The fact she got to share her news with him, that he was right then, waiting for her to come back to him, was so amazing. Gods, she loved him.

It was crazy how quickly he had become the most important thing in her world. But then again, maybe not. They were fated mates. It was destiny. But even without that, she loved Brock more than she had ever loved anyone or anything in her entire life.

It was all really that straightforward. After all the misunderstandings and miscommunications, finally admitting they loved each other and consummating that love made everything else seem trivial.

Ariella was pleased that she won, but she actually felt sorry for her workplace nemesis. She hoped Cornelia would find her own mate someday and stop living so maliciously.

Dang, she really wanted Brock. Like now.

Wanted to discuss what had happened with him, but he would probably be at work now.

Sad rawr.

"Hey Ari, someone's here for you," Toni shouted from her own desk as Ari's head shot up.

She guessed she didn't have to wait at all. Striding down the hall was her sexy as sin Dire Wolf, his laser like focus narrowed on her. Ariella felt a purr build inside her chest as the pine fresh scent of her one and only invaded her senses.

Putting a lid on her little kitty, she hurried across the room and met him halfway. He uncrossed his arms, a knowing grin on his handsome face.

"Hey, there," she said.

"Hi yourself, hellcat. Did you win?" he asked excitedly.

He grabbed her hands loosely in his. The hold was casual, but she noted the flare of his nostrils and the heat in his gaze. His Wolf was pushing him just as fiercely as her she-Cat. She bit her lip and nodded as he grabbed her bag and tugged her out the door.

"Yes! I knew it. Congrats, minx," he growled, giving her a backbreaking hug, and she loved every second of it.

"Thank you. Come on. The boss said I could

leave now," she said, thrilled he was there and seemed so proud of her.

"Good," he growled. "Sorry, I just couldn't wait to see you," he said and pulled her outside and tossed her things into the saddlebag on the side of his Harley.

He backed her up against the bike, making her swoon with one of his patented kisses designed to make her fall to her knees in worship of the man's skill alone.

Would it always be this good, she wondered? Not at all surprised when he nodded. Their matebond was warm and bright, pulsing all around them like a living, breathing connection. It was quite possible he heard her thoughts.

"Always," he growled, confirming her suspicions.

"Mmm, I love you," she moaned and whimpered when he pulled away.

"Love you too, mate. Let's get out of here before we give everyone a show," he grunted and reached out, giving her ass a little pinch that had her yelping and jumping to get into her seat behind him.

It wasn't easy in her skirt, but she managed just fine. Anything to get closer to him.

"You know, that hurt," she whined as he fastened the helmet on her pretty little head.

"Don't worry, minx. I'll kiss it better, I promise."

"You better," she said and squeezed his middle with her arms snug around his waist.

It was his turn to yelp when her hands moved a little lower, stroking his impressive length. Brock growled playfully before pulling them back up and over his belt.

"I'd like to get there in one piece, hellcat," he grunted and revved the engine loudly.

"So, who's running the kitchen?"

"I left everything in Cole's capable hands. He can answer any questions the cooks have, besides Carlo is almost ready to be head chef on his own. I needed some time off with my mate."

"Yeah? How about two weeks," she said and couldn't hide the pride in her voice.

"For real? That's the prize? Yes!!"

"I won fair and square. Run away with me to an island?" She yelled her question over the roar of his Harley as he zoomed down the highway towards Blue Valley.

His low-slung sports car was a dream of a ride, but Ariella loved being on the back of his motorcycle even more. It was big and loud, but like everything else he did, Brock was positively fluid and thorough in his handling of the finely tuned machinery.

He revved the engine and sped up, stopping when they got to the Pack house. The fact was, Ari would go anywhere the big man led, but she was a tad disappointed at the idea of sharing him just then.

"Don't worry," he said, seeming to read her mind again. "You get me all to yourself later, but after your announcement, this couldn't wait. I want to do things in order."

"What things, Brock?"

She followed him inside the Pack house, confused and amazed at the same time. It was early in the evening, her workday had flown by, and the Spring air was crisp and cool. Thor sat in the living room with a thick book in his hands. The bald, tattooed giant grunted as he closed the book and looked from Brock to her, then back again.

"You sure, bro?"

"Yes," Brock said, and the context went right over her head.

"I'll get the box. You call the others."

"Brock? What's going on?"

"Ariella, I know I've said it before, but I love you," he whispered against her lips. "More than I ever thought possible. We have already claimed each other, but for my people, there is more."

"More?"

"Yes. You see, when a Dire Wolf finds his fated mate, there is a ritual that needs to happen to make things permanent."

"A ritual?" she said with wonder, touching his face with cautious fingers, unwilling to break the spell he was weaving around them.

He was so damn beautiful her breath got stuck in her chest. Ariella did not know what he meant, but she was all for it. Whatever she needed to do to be his forever, she was game. She'd assumed things were permanent, after all, they'd claimed one another, but who really knew in this day and age what permanent meant.

"It means forever, hellcat. I'll never let you go. I love you. You are a part of me, and my testament to that and to us is this," he said.

Brock nodded towards where Thor was now kneeling on the floor of the living room with a strange wooden box in his hands. It was the answer to every single one of her spoken and unspoken prayers. She loved Brock Laurent with every last piece of her heart and soul, to have him confess his feelings to her was like a dream.

"Are you sure?"

"Ariella Golden, I have never been surer about anything in all my life."

Pride and love beat through her veins like blood, a mad temp that made her breathless. Ariella reached up and kissed her mate, loving the gentleness she found there. He was so hard and focused when he was working or concentrating, but she got this part of him. His softness was only for her, and she adored it all the more for that reason.

"I love you," she said.

"I love you too, mate."

CHAPTER 15

B rock gave his beautiful little hellcat a reassuring kiss, then tilted his head back and loosed a howl that each member of his Pack in the vicinity was sure to hear. Thor was almost finished with preparations for the marking ritual, and he needed Derrick with him.

"You see, love," Brock explained. "Thor is what we Dire Wolves call *favored by the gods*. He will see our path and engrave it on my skin."

He'd caught Ariella eying him curiously as Brock unbuttoned the thick flannel shirt he'd been wearing. He pulled that off, and the tank top he had on underneath next. Tugging it up and over his head from the back.

He'd been thinking about this moment ever since

he'd met Ariella. It was an honor he had never expected to experience and the fact that she accepted and welcomed him into her life, body, heart, and soul, made him the luckiest fucker on the planet.

"yeah, what he means is Thor's a bit touched," explained Phoenix with a wicked wink. The big man came in and untied his apron, tossing it on the couch, before high-fiving Ari.

"Shut up, you idiot," Sheila said, following behind him. She smacked her Pack mate upside the head to Brock's unending amusement and Ari's sweet giggle.

Fuck, he loved it when she was happy and made a vow to always try to make her laugh. As their Beta, Brock had some authority over his Pack, but why would he want to stop some good old fashioned sassing? Especially when his own mate added that little pinch of sass in his life, he'd never known he needed.

It was quite an event, bringing a mate into the fold, but he had never been surer of anything in all the world. His little feline was all he had ever wanted and, now that he had her, he wasn't letting go.

"Hey, y'all tried to start without me!" Lucy accused as she padded into the room on slippered feet with a bowl of popcorn in one hand and a large, frosty milkshake in the other.

"Dammit, woman, wait a second and I'll carry all that for you," Derrick growled from the other room.

He followed behind her with a roll of paper towels, and the ever present glass of iced water she'd been keeping on hand the last week or so. For some reason, the expectant mama couldn't get enough fluids in her diet.

"Now, Ari, Brock is gonna go over there and kneel in front of Thor. Thor is going to channel the fates and mumble some such shit we won't understand, then he will get a vision. That vision is Brock's true heart and his path now that he's found you. He's gonna ink that shit on your hunk a burnin' Wolf. Ain't it great?" Lucy grinned and sucked some thick chocolate milkshake through her straw.

"Really? I didn't know," Ari whispered, and it seemed right that she had.

Pride filled him at her knowing intuition. She was one hell of a woman, and he would do everything it took to keep her safe and protected, cherished, and loved for the rest of their entire lives.

Thor lifted the first bamboo needle and dipped it in the jar of magicked ink and Brock felt his eyes glowing with his Wolf as the ritual began. His Pack mates closed in around him, including Ari, who stood just in front. Locking eyes with her, he saw her love shining out like a beacon, calling him home, and he knew he was home wherever he was with her.

She was the central part of his circle now and as tears welled in her eyes, he knew those tears were full of love and pride. He remained focused on her, on their bond as Thor worked. Brock knew his eyes would be overcast with the trance-like state he was in, channeling the Fates and bringing that vision from his mind and onto his Pack mate's skin.

The image was in the center of Brock's wide back and though he had the odd tattoo, this was the first major piece the Wolf had ever sat for. It took over an hour, but he was strong and steadfast. The rags soaked with his blood that Thor had mopped up as he etched into his skin with the sharp needles sat in a pile.

When he lifted his hand and dropped the needle, Weylin and Phoenix rushed to Thor's side. The huge Dire Wolf Shifter sometimes got drained after a long process, such as this had been. Brock was exhausted, too. The inking process was not a matter of merely getting tattooed during this ritual, it was like having someone wriggling around inside your very soul and pulling out what he saw there, scratching it onto his skin for everyone to see.

The very idea was astounding. A fantasy brought to life. Thor was a legend among his kind, and Brock sucked in a breath and whispered his gratitude. His beautiful mate came forward, kneeling before him and placing his hands on her shoulders to steady him.

"Are you okay?" she asked anxiously.

"Yes, now that I have you, hellcat," he replied easily. Brock grinned and kissed the hand she'd brought up to caress his face.

"Damn."

"Wow," Sheila gasped.

"That is, really, I am just," the Alpha fem stuttered, and then Lucy started bawling.

"Come here, kitten," Derrick scooped up his wife and held her while she cried.

"I am so proud of you two, Brock," she said through tears, and he nodded at his Alpha fem, then looked back at Ariella.

"What is it?" he asked and turned around.

Her gasp made him nervous, but he waited for her to speak.

"Oh wow, Pookie. I mean, I knew you loved me,

but wow," she said, and he heard her grin in her voice.

"Pookie?" Phoenix asked to the stifled snickers and snorts of the rest of them.

"Stuff it, asshat," Brock growled at him, then asked his mate to describe the tattoo.

"There's a circle of like hieroglyphs or runes, a heart, a stone, a star, a moon, and at the center is a White Wolf lying near a stream, beside him is a Lioness. They're side by side, looking out to the future, together. Oh Brock, it's beautiful," she said, and this time it was tears thickening her beloved whisper.

Turning, he took her hands and pulled her into the circle of his arms. His skin was tender, but as a Shifter he had already begun to heal. He wasn't worried about it, not when Ariella wrapped her arms around him and hugged him close to her heart. It was the only place in the world he ever wanted to be.

Afterwards, they invited her sisters and mother over to the restaurant, where they held a celebratory meal over their mating. It was like the Shifter equivalent of an engagement party. Fitting, since at the end of dinner Brock surprised his mate with a solitary sapphire in a band of yellow gold and a marriage proposal that had every female in the place teary eyed.

"I got a question for you, Ariella," he said and kneeled down to her wide, golden-eyed stare. The entire room had gone still, and Brock took the ring out of his pocket and held it up to her. A small token of his love and esteem.

"I know I fucked this up in the beginning, but I promise to spend every second of every day from now until the end of time making it up to you. I don't care what we do, where we go, as long as I am with you, I have everything I will ever need. I love you. We are paired in the Shifter world, but I want you everywhere I can get you, hellcat. So, it would make me the happiest man on the planet if you agreed to be my wife. Will you marry me?" he asked.

"Get up," Ari whispered.

She sniffed, and Brock stood slowly. Had he gotten this wrong? He wondered that for all of two seconds before she vaulted into his arms and yelled the word yes like a banshee ringing in his ears.

It was the best fucking sound he'd ever heard. Except for Ariella's moans whenever she was eating. And he vowed to be there for every meal from then on.

Mine. Mate. Wife.

EPILOGUE

"Greetings and Welcome to Moongate Island, Mr. and Mrs. Laurent. I am Mr. Gordon, the manager here at Stein Luxury Resorts, please allow me to show you to your rooms," the smiling hotel manager said.

Ariella grinned up at her new husband and mate while a bellhop wrangled their luggage. Brock returned her smile with an affectionate kiss on her brow and took her hand as they followed him to their honeymoon suite.

Eat Well Live Proud, having heard of her sudden nuptials, had upgraded her prize and sent them on the two-week honeymoon she'd been dreaming about since she was a cub.

Of course, Ms. Pierce was hoping she would land

them more of the international hotel's business—but this was not a working holiday.

After they found themselves alone, Ariella walked over to where her husband was standing near one of the floor-to-ceiling, one-way windows. She licked her lips nervously.

Being seductive was not something that came naturally to her, and yet there was nothing more instinctive than wanting to please her mate. The flowy white dress she'd worn on the private jet he'd rented them felt too constricting on her skin and her Lioness pressed against her, egging her on.

"Brock?"

"Yeah, love?"

He turned, but stilled instantly when he noticed her heavy-lidded stare. She knew he could sense her mood, scent her need, and Ariella reached for the straps to her dress and tipped them off her shoulders, tugging the elastic material down until it pooled at her feet. Brock's soft growl was audible in the otherwise empty room as he stared at her in the skimpy little lace thong and bra she wore, just for the occasion.

"Mine," he growled as his legs ate the distance between them.

There was nothing better than kissing Brock,

except maybe making love to Brock. Her mate was just as hungry for her as she was for him. He ripped off his clothing and lifted her in his arms. The bed was too far away, it seemed, but they did manage to make it to the thick rug that sat on the warm wooden floor.

"Oh Brock," she moaned as his tongue found her heated center.

Ariella draped her legs over his shoulder while her mate suckled her sex with expert flicks of his tongue. When he growled, she practically went cross-eyed with pleasure. Who needed a vibrator when her mate could rumble against her clit with the best of them?

In minutes she was coming, and her greedy Wolf insisted on sucking down every last drop of her juices before he slid up her body. Good thing she was already ready for round two.

"It gets better every time," she moaned as he positioned his heavy cock against her swollen lips.

"That's cause you're perfect, hellcat," he growled and mashed his lips to hers as he invaded her slick flesh.

The perfect pressure of his girthy length stroking her had Ariella spiraling out of control in mere moments. Her body belonged to him. It was as if it recognized the pleasure he could bring instinctively. She scratched him with her claws, loving the fact that each time she claimed him, she felt their bond grow and strengthen.

"Love you, mate," he groaned as he flexed his hips, swirling against her pubis until they were both drowning in ecstasy.

Hours later, after they were both sated, Ariella and Brock headed down to the beach for an evening swim. He'd ordered them a secluded meal to be served on the shore in a special private cabana he'd rented.

"This is gorgeous," she sighed the sentiment, so happy she could damn near burst.

"It is," he replied and kissed her head, wrapping his arm around her as they lounged in the two-person chaise and watched the waves through the open section of the sheer curtains that hung around their private cabana.

Everything was perfect. Ariella finally had her mate. She was thoroughly claimed and mated, and so happy she could hardly believe this was her life. Even better, she got him all to herself for two whole weeks of loving.

"What are you thinking, hellcat?"

"Mmmm. Just thinking how wonderful it is to be

here with you, in paradise, alone," she murmured, raising her lips for one of his toe-curling kisses.

Ariella spoke too soon, she thought as the curtains to the left of their chaise suddenly burst open and Patricia Golden ran right into their private little honeymoon.

"There you two are," the Lioness said, ducking behind their lounge chair.

"Mom?! What are you doing here?'

"Look, honey, you gotta hide me. He followed me here!"

"I don't believe this," Ariella moaned, and Brock blinked from mother to daughter.

"Is that any way to talk to your mother? After all I did to get you two together? Dosing you and setting this big puppy up to fall for you. You would think I'd get a little bit of help when I ask for it," she growled, and turned in shock when a billowing roar sounded just outside the cabana followed by a massive, silver streaked male Lion.

"Now, Donovan," she said and ran behind Ariella.

"King Donovan? Mom, what the hell is going on?" she asked her mother, but the woman was too busy trying to back away from the obviously angry male, who just shifted back to his very naked, very human skin.

"*Ohmygawdmyeyes*," Ariella yowled.

Brock tossed the man a towel, to which King Donovan Crowley nodded his thanks.

"I will tell you what is going on, stepdaughter. My *mate* keeps running out on me!" the King of the Blue Valley Pride roared loudly and Ariella and Brock both busted out laughing.

"You two are mates?" Brock asked.

"Yes, we exchanged bites two weeks ago and ever since I haven't seen hide nor hair of her," he pointed accusingly.

"Mom! Is that why you've been so upset?" Ariella asked and crouched next to her mother, who was wringing her hands in her lap.

"I just didn't want to lose myself to some dominant pussy! Look, I'm not going to change, Donovan, even if you are the king!"

To that, the king kneeled in front of his mate and Brock and Ariella stood up and slowly backed away.

"I don't want you to change. I love you, Pat, always have," he said and smiled, and Ariella's mother smiled back. Then they were kissing, and it was time for Ari and her mate to haul ass out of there.

"Ari, um, I think, maybe we should—" Brock began.

"I hear you, loud and clear," she said and grabbed his hand.

She loved her mother, but this was *her* honeymoon. After a few phone calls, Ariella and Brock moved to a private cottage on the beach, away from other hotel guests, and they transferred the other suite to her mother's name.

"You good with this," she asked Brock as they lay in a tangle of arms and legs in the hammock outside their private hut.

"Hellcat, I am perfect as long as I have you."

"Yeah?"

"Yes. I love you, mate."

"Love you, too."

With that said, Ariella reached around his superb body, and she pinched him right on his gloriously muscled ass. With a loud shriek, she jumped up and ran, her own naked ass jiggling the whole way down their private section of the beach, hoping her mate would follow.

Brock let out a playful Dire Wolf howl, then follow her, he did.

The end.

Liked this story? Want more Dire Wolf Mates?
Grab the next book, Kickin' Sass, at https://www.cdgorri.
com/books/kickin-sass.
Or
Follow the whole series at https://www.cdgorri.com/seres/
dire-wolf-mates.

Thank you and happy reading!

BEWARE... HERE BE DRAGONS!

The Falk Clan Tales began as my stories surrounding four dragon Brothers and how they find their one true mates, but when a long lost brother arrives on the scene, followed by a few more Shifters…what can I say? The more the merrier!

Each Dragon's chest is marked with his rose, the magical link to his heart and his magic. They each have a matching gemstone to go with it.

She's given up on love. But he's just begun.

In The Dragon's Valentine we meet the eldest Falk brother, Callius. He is on a mission to find a Castle and his one true mate, one he can trust with his diamond rose....

His heart is frozen. Can she change his mind about love?

In The Dragon's Christmas Gift our attention shifts to Alexsander, the youngest brother of the four. He has resigned himself to a life alone, until he meets *her*.

Some wounds run deep. Can a Dragon's heart be unbroken?

The Dragon's Heart is the story of Edric Falk who has vowed never to love again, but that changes when he meets his feisty mate, Joselyn Curacao.

She just wants a little fun. He's looking for a lifetime.

We finally meet Nikolai Falk and his sexy Shifter mate in The Dragon's Secret.

She doesn't believe in fairytales, until a Dragon comes knocking on her door.

Meet Castor Falk, the long lost brother of our original four Dragons, and his sassy mate Josette. The Dragon's Treasure is full of adventure and laughs.

Nothing can surprise this six hundred-year-old Dragon, except maybe her.

Devine Graystone meets his match in Sunny Daye, an irrepressible Wolf Shifter with a heart of gold. Read their story in The Dragon's Surprise.

He's a hardcore realist until she dares him to dream.

Nicholas Gravestone doesn't know what to think when he spies Minerva Lykos on the property his Dragon covets. Can this unlikely pair come to a truce? Find out in The Dragon's Dream.

Thanks for reading. xoxo

    *Dragon Mates & Dragon Mates 2 boxed sets are now available in hardcover, paperback, and ebook.

HAVE YOU MET MY BEARS?

Looking for a Paranormal Romance series that is loads of growly fun?

Meet the Barvale Clan first in the Bear Claw Tales! A complete shifter romance series about 4 brothers who discover and need to win their fated mates!

Followed by two more spin off series, the Barvale Clan Tales and the Barvale Holiday Tales!

No cliffhangers. Steamy PNR fun.
Go and read your next happily ever after today!

OTHER TITLES BY C.D. GORRI

Other Titles by C.D. Gorri

Paranormal Romance Books:

Macconwood Pack Novel Series:

Charley's Christmas Wolf: A Macconwood Pack Novel 1

Cat's Howl: A Macconwood Pack Novel 2

Code Wolf: A Macconwood Pack Novel 3

The Witch and The Werewolf: A Macconwood Pack Novel 4

To Claim a Wolf: A Macconwood Pack Novel 5

Conall's Mate: A Macconwood Pack Novel 6

Her Solstice Wolf: A Macconwood Pack Novel 7

Werewolf Fever: A Macconwood Pack Novel 8

Also available in 2 boxed sets:

The Macconwood Pack Volume 1

The Macconwood Pack Volume 2

Macconwood Pack Tales Series:

Wolf Bride: The Story of Ailis and Eoghan A

Macconwood Pack Tale 1

Summer Bite: A Macconwood Pack Tale 2

His Winter Mate: A Macconwood Pack Tale 3

Snow Angel: A Macconwood Pack Tale 4

Charley's Baby Surprise: A Macconwood Pack Tale 5

Home for the Howlidays: A Macconwood Pack Tale 6

A Silver Wedding: A Macconwood Pack Tale 7

Mine Furever: A Macconwood Pack Tale 8

A Furry Little Christmas: A Macconwood Pack Tale 9

Also available in two boxed sets:

The Macconwood Pack Tales Volume 1

Shifters Furever: The Macconwood Pack Tales Volume 2

<u>The Falk Clan Tales:</u>

The Dragon's Valentine: A Falk Clan Novel 1

The Dragon's Christmas Gift: A Falk Clan Novel 2

The Dragon's Heart: A Falk Clan Novel 3

The Dragon's Secret: A Falk Clan Novel 4

The Dragon's Treasure: A Falk Clan Novel 5

The Dragon's Surprise: A Falk Clan Novel 6

The Dragon's Dream: A Falk Clan Novel 7

Dragon Mates: The Falk Clan Series Boxed Set Books 1-4

Dragon Mates 2: The Falk Clan Series Boxed Set Books

<u>The Bear Claw Tales:</u>

Bearly Breathing: A Bear Claw Tale 1

Bearly There: A Bear Claw Tale 2

Bearly Tamed: A Bear Claw Tale 3

Bearly Mated: A Bear Claw Tale 4

Also available in a boxed set:

The Complete Bear Claw Tales (Books 1-4)

<u>The Barvale Clan Tales:</u>

Polar Opposites: The Barvale Clan Tales 1

Polar Outbreak: The Barvale Clan Tales 2

Polar Compound: A Barvale Clan Tale 3

Polar Curve: A Barvale Clan Tale 4

Also available in a boxed set:

The Barvale Clan Tales (Books 1-4)

<u>Barvale Holiday Tales:</u>

A Bear For Christmas

Hers To Bear

Thank You Beary Much

Bearing Gifts

Also available in a boxed set:

The Barvale Holiday Tales (Books 1-3)

<u>Purely Paranormal Romance Books:</u>

Marked by the Devil: Purely Paranormal Romance Books

Mated to the Dragon King: Purely Paranormal Romance Books

Claimed by the Demon: Purely Paranormal Romance Books

Christmas with a Devil, a Dragon King, & a Demon: Purely Paranormal Romance Books

Vampire Lover: Purely Paranormal Romance Books

Grizzly Lover: Purely Paranormal Romance Books

Christmas With Her Chupacabra: Purely Paranormal Romance Books

Purely Paranormal Romance Books Anthology

<u>The Wardens of Terra:</u>

Bound by Air: The Wardens of Terra Book 1

Star Kissed: A Wardens of Terra Short

Waterlocked: The Wardens of Terra Book 2

Moon Kissed: A Wardens of Terra Short

*Now in a boxed set and in audio!

<u>The Maverick Pride Tales:</u>

Purrfectly Mated

Purrfectly Kissed

Purrfectly Trapped

Purrfectly Caught

Purrfectly Naughty

Purrfectly Bound

Purrfectly Paired

<u>Dire Wolf Mates:</u>

Shake That Sass

Breaking Sass

Pinch of Sass

Kickin' Sass

<u>Wyvern Protection Unit:</u>

Gift Wrapped Protector: WPU 1

<u>Standalones:</u>

The Enforcer

Blood Song: A Sanguinem Council Book

Spring Fling (co-written with P. Mattern)

<u>EveL Worlds:</u>

Chinchilla and the Devil: A FUCN'A Book

Sammi and the Jersey Bull: A FUCN'A Book

Mouse and the Ball: A FUCN'A Book

Chicken and the Paparazzi: A FUCN'A Book

<u>The Guardians of Chaos:</u>

Wolf Shield: Guardians of Chaos Book1

Dragon Shield: Guardians of Chaos Book 2

Stallion Shield: Guardians of Chaos Book 3

Panther Shield: Guardians of Chaos 4

Witch Shield: Guardians of Chaos 5

Vampire Shield: Guardians of Chaos 6

Guardians of Chaos Volume 1 Books 1-3

Guardians of Chaos Volume 2 Books 4-6

Howl's Romance

Mated to the Werewolf Next Door: A Howl's Romance

The Tiger King's Christmas Bride

Claiming His Virgin Mate: Howls Romance

Twice Mated Tales

Doubly Claimed

Doubly Bound

Doubly Tied

Twice Mated Tales Anthology

Hearts of Stone Series

Shifter Mountain: Hearts of Stone 1

Shifter City: Hearts of Stone 2

Shifter Village: Hearts of Stone 3

Hearts of Stone Books 1-3 Anthology

Accidentally Undead Series

Fangs For Nothin'

<u>Moongate Island Tales</u>

Moongate Island Mate

Moongate Island Christmas Claim

<u>Mated in Hope Falls</u>

Mated by Moonlight

<u>Speed Dating with the Denizens of the Underworld</u>

Ash: Speed Dating with the Denizens of Underworld

Arachne: Speed Dating with the Denizens of Underworld

Asterion: Speed Dating with the Denizens of Underworld

<u>Hungry Fur Love</u>

Hungry Like Her Wolf: Magic and Mayhem Universe

Hungry For Her Bear: Magic and Mayhem Universe

<u>Shifters Unleashed Boxed Sets</u>

<u>Island Stripe Pride</u>

Tiger Claimed

Tiger Denied

Tiger Rejected

*Tiger Tales Anthology

<u>NYC Shifter Tales</u>

Cuff Linked

Sealed Fate

A Howlin' Good Fairytale Retelling

Sweet As Candy (single edition coming soon)

Coming Soon:

Hungry As Her Python: Magic and Mayhem Universe

Bearly Friends

If The Shoe Fits: A Howlin' Good Fairytale Retelling

The Wolf's Winter Wish: A Macconwood Pack Tale

The Hybrid Assassin

For Fangs Sake

Tempted By Her Protector: WPU 2

Alien Protector: WPU 3

Unexpected Protector: WPU 4

Thrilled By Her Protector: WPU 5

###

Young Adult Urban Fantasy Books:

Wolf Moon: A Grazi Kelly Novel Book 1

Hunter Moon: A Grazi Kelly Novel Book 2

Rebel Moon: A Grazi Kelly Novel Book 3

Winter Moon: A Grazi Kelly Novel Book 4

Chasing The Moon: A Grazi Kelly Short 5

Blood Moon: A Grazi Kelly Novel 6

*Get all 6 books NOW AVAILABLE IN A BOXED SET:

The Complete Grazi Kelly Novel Series

Casting Magic: The Angela Tanner Files 1

Keeping Magic: The Angela Tanner Files 2

<u>G'Witches Magical Mysteries Series</u>

Co-written with P. Mattern

G'Witches

G'Witches 2: The Harpy Harbinger

G'Witches 3: Summoning Secrets

EXCERPT FROM PURRFECTLY MATED

How the fuck did I wind up here?

It was all Elissa could do not to slam her face down on the table as she pondered that question for the umpteenth time since leaving her cozy Hoboken apartment to go on this so called date.

"So, babe," the over-stuffed, heavily-cologned, and downright fugly man said.

Her date of the evening looked like something out of a bad sitcom as he tried to lean over the stained tablecloth of the rundown hotel buffet room, he'd driven two hours to get to. Waggling his caterpillar-like eyebrows, he gave her the once over and Elissa's skin crawled.

Oh, hell no.

"I got a room upstairs, you know, for *after*," he told her, nodding his head, and biting his lower lip in a manner she assumed he thought was provocative.

At best, it was nauseating.

FML.

How was this guy Elissa's date for the evening? What had she done to deserve this?

Little Gianni. Yup, that was how he'd introduced himself. And here she was. On a blind date with a guy who had the word 'little' in front of his name.

Well, what did she expect? Roses and champagne? In this economy? She didn't know where Cinder-fucking-ella got her prince, but it sure as fuck wasn't in Jersey.

Elissa could only blame herself for agreeing to go on this blind date. Initially, the whole Little Gianni fiasco had been intended for her roommate.

Wait a second. Scratch that thought.

It *was* all Gretchen's fault. That ungrateful cow!

She tried to play it off like she was some sweet little homegrown maiden. Oh, just wait till Elissa got home. Gretchen was never going to hear the end of it.

She owed Elissa. Big time. Like a whole month of

washing the dishes big time. The rat trap they shared in her hometown of Hoboken was all the two women could afford, and for the most part, they got along just fine.

In fact, they'd grown to be close friends over the three years they'd lived together. It was the only reason she'd ever agreed to this date from Hell.

Elissa sighed and looked over at Little Gianni. Maybe he wasn't all that bad?

"*BEEEELLLLLLLLCHHH!* 'Scuse me, doll. Better out, am I right?"

Gianni winked and Elissa wished for a black hole to open up and swallow her up right through the floor.

OMFG.

The man just burped out loud like he was in a frat boy belting contest, only those days passed him up about thirty years ago.

For fuck's sake. Gretchen, you so owe me.

Elissa cursed her roommate and tried not to groan. But Little Gianni wasn't quite done. The grown ass man lifted his leg and let one rip.

Right. Fucking. There.

Elissa was going to die before the end of the night.

Literally.

This is what you get when you do a friend a favor without asking for details! Idiota!

The voice of her Italian grandmother sounded in her brain. She tried to ignore it, willing herself not to wince at the man while he sucked air, and who knows what else, noisily through his coffee-stained teeth.

Ew. So gross.

That was the perfect word to describe it. The only word, in fact. The entire date was just so fucking gross. She still couldn't believe her sweet little roommate from Iowa, *Gretchen Kaepernick*, she of the wispy hair and baby blues, had set her up with this guy!

What the actual fuck was up with that?

Little Gianni was a slob. Actually, he looked just like her Uncle Nico, and that was not a good thing. Seriously, not good at all.

He wore his hair slicked back in a too tight pony-tail that emphasized his rapidly receding hairline. As if that wasn't enough to put her off, he was sporting an enormous paunch. Now, being a curvy girl, Elissa appreciated food and was in no way against men showing the same appreciation.

She liked bigger men. Always had. But bigger did not mean you had to be sloppy. Little Gianni's stomach was literally hanging out from under a tight tan golf shirt that had definitely seen better days.

The man didn't even look like he had ever played a sport of any kind. With it, he wore brown polyester pants that were three inches above his ankles and unbuttoned at the waist.

He didn't look like he tried at all for this date. What kind of guy did that? His shirt collar was bent and wrinkled, and all three buttons were open to his chest, revealing a mat of oily, dark hair and pimples.

Somehow, he'd managed to tuck the back of the shirt in, but the front simply would not hold in that stomach. What worried her more were the tight brown pants.

As he sat back and stretched, she wondered if she should take cover. They looked like they were one bite from exploding off his body. Elissa shuddered at the image.

Please God, if You have an ounce of mercy, don't let that happen, she prayed.

"Hang on, doll, I gotta take this," he said, and turned to answer his cell phone.

It was ringing to the tune of '70s disco music she

hadn't heard since the last family reunion. Her eyes kept going to the huge stain on the front of his shirt. It was a little game she liked to call *what the hell is that.*

Coffee, she guessed.

"Up your ass, Bruno. I gotta have it by Monday," he cursed into the receiver.

Elissa winced at the spectacle he was making of them both. There were only a handful of people there, but still.

Deep breaths.

Ew. Maybe not.

She coughed as the strong body spray, that he'd obviously used a ton of in lieu of a shower, bad move in her opinion, invaded her lungs.

Oh, this was so bad.

Elissa was, by no means, a snob. But this guy looked like he'd stepped out of a bad 1980s mafia spoof film. What's worse, he kept smacking his lips together as he hung up the phone and looked her over from head to chest.

Thank fuck for the table, she thought, wishing she could hide her bosoms from his view.

"Ssssss," he hissed, like it was sexy or something.

She just grimaced. Elissa might be able to forgive a lot of quirks, but she hated mouth noises. Really hated them. It was a super pet peeve of hers. Never mind his totally inappropriate and unwelcomed leer.

She started counting the minutes, willing the date to be over already. Plenty of people would tell her she shouldn't be so choosy, but really? She was not this desperate.

Not yet anyway.

So, she was curvy and a little mouthy too. But was it wrong to want a man with good table manners? Even if men were thin on the ground for someone like her.

As a chef, she'd worked in a lot of restaurants and even as a personal cook for professional couples. She'd seen her fair share of unhappy couples and downright uncomfortable marriages. But as far as she was concerned, all relationships went downhill when good table manners were dismissed.

Good manners were merely a sign that a person was thoughtful and respectful. At least, that was what Nonna had told her. Gianni here had clearly missed that lesson as a child. Elissa had to work not to groan in disgust as he slurped a raw clam down his gullet.

Shudder.

Was there no end to his feeding? That's what it reminded her of. Feeding time at the zoo.

OMG. That was rude, she scolded herself. But it wasn't like she said it out loud.

All she wanted to do was go home. At least she was comfortable. *She'd* worn her softest pair of black leggings for this disaster date, paired with one of her favorite tunics on top.

It was dark green with tiny black buttons down the front and showed just the right amount of cleavage. She'd gone for neat and tidy as opposed to downright sexy.

Good call, in her opinion. Elissa looked perfectly fine for a nice *getting to know you* dinner, which is what she thought she was getting when her roommate asked her to step in for her on a blind date that one of her best client's had set up for her.

Elissa shuddered now, thinking how good old Gianni here would've reacted to the red dress and heels she'd contemplated before checking the weather report.

Gulp.

The lewd man was already salivating, and she was so not having it. Fending off his unwanted advances was not how she wanted to finish the night.

Ew again.

Elissa shivered, slightly chilled despite the fact

they were indoors. It was a cold, gloomy evening, and the forecast called for even more rain later that night. Not at all unusual for this time of year in the Garden State.

November was always chilly in the evenings, rainy too. Elissa tended to run warm, but she was glad she'd brought a jacket with her. Especially since her date refused to turn the heat on in the car.

When she'd asked, he'd looked offended and told her it wasted gas.

Um. Okay.

She checked her phone. It was only seven o'clock, but the two hour drive was still ahead of them. Maybe they could make it home before ten if they left soon.

Ugh. Did he just blow his nose?

"Allergies, doll. Say, you gonna eat that?" he asked before scooping a fry from her dish and swallowing it down.

Elissa was gonna kill her roomie. Gretchen was a hair and nail stylist. A lot of her clients were elderly, and they just loved her. They were always offering to set her up on blind dates with their nephews and grandsons.

Mostly, the sweet old ladies were kind. They swore they could find her curvy roommate the right man, assuming she was single because she was new to town. Well, when Elissa got home tonight, she was going to tell Gretchen she needed to fire the old lady who set this date up from being her client.

Like *ASAP*.

No one who liked Gretchen would've sent her out with this guy. Gianni reached over and touched her hand and Elissa pulled back, reaching for the napkin.

Gross.

"I sure hope you ain't a cold one, doll," he said, shaking his head.

"What?"

"Ain't gonna matter. I know just what you need, doll."

She was still wiping the greasy residue he'd transferred to her skin from the food he ate sans utensils. This was too much. Elissa was beyond uncomfortable with all the leering and bad attempts at innuendo.

Plus, she was starving. One look at the dump he'd taken her to, and she knew she could never eat there. The chef in her wouldn't allow it.

To think they drove two hours for this! She'd practically frozen to death in his maroon Cadillac, listening to a CD of the Rat Pack, while Gianni crooned loudly, and off key, to the music.

Normally, she was a fan of the famous group of legendary singers. Having grown up in Hoboken, she couldn't not be a Sinatra fan. Though, to be honest, Dean Martin had always been her favorite.

Still, Elissa was a firm believer that there were just some people you did not try to imitate. Especially not if you were Little Gianni. While he was belting his heart out, he'd been trying to get his right hand on her thigh. She'd asked him politely to stop.

Twice.

Then she'd been forced to try something a little more drastic. Like spilling her hot tea on the offending hand the third time he'd tried it. Finally, he'd removed his hand from her leg. Not making a fourth attempt, which she was grateful for.

Elissa should've taken that behavior as a sign and gotten out of the car. But no. She'd wanted to do Gretchen a solid. So, against her better judgement, she gave the creep another chance.

Idiota, her grandmother's voice echoed in her brain again.

The old woman had loved her. Elissa knew that without a doubt. She'd raised her after her own parents had passed on in a tragic automobile accident when Elissa was just twelve.

Her grandmother was a no-nonsense kind of lady who dished out priceless wisdom with brutally honest insights. It was the same way she dished out huge bowls of pasta with her amazing meatballs and homemade sauce. Not to mention a side order of back-breaking hugs that Elissa still missed.

Nonna cooked like that all the time. She made a huge pot of sauce every weekend, and she was happy to serve it to Elissa and her teammates and friends, especially after games and tournaments.

Soccer had been her sport of choice, and cooking had soon become her favorite hobby. Her grandmother had encouraged her in both pursuits. Guiding her in one and cheering her on in the other. Elissa still missed her terribly.

"Hey babe, ain't you gonna eat nothin'? You know they charge twenty dollars just to sit down," Little Gianni interrupted her train of thought.

Elissa was forced to turn her mind back to the present, which unfortunately included watching, *and hearing,* him as he sucked on his teeth and stuffed another breaded shrimp down his throat.

"I'm fine," she answered with a polite smile plastered on her face.

Just get home, Lissa. Just get him to take you home.

Elissa closed her eyes when he looked back down at his dish. Thank God for small favors, she mused. At least he was more interested in eating at the moment.

He'd taken her to the rattiest looking hotel and casino she'd ever seen in her life. And the buffet room?

Ew.

Seriously, the place had to be violating at least a dozen health codes. When Gianni had said Atlantic City, she'd thought at least the atmosphere would be exciting. But they were so far from the real glitz and entertainment, they might as well be anywhere else.

She sighed, looking at the plate she'd made for herself. Elissa couldn't even fake an interest in the food. As a chef, it was hard enough to dine out.

She was always judging the food, the service, the ingredients. How could she not? It was her business. And that was when the food was good!

This was not good. Not at all.

She'd been to hospitals that served better food. Old yellow lights buzzed and blinked around the buffet, giving it an abandoned kind of feel. The menu was made up of mostly frozen then fried or baked cuisine.

Reheated actually. It was like a giant TV dinner buffet where every item was previously frozen when already cooked and warmed up in an oven.

It was the kind of food sold cheap at restaurant supply stores in bulk. Yeah, this was much worse than hospital food, in her opinion.

There was a worn carpet on the floor, a handful of scattered tables in the dining room, elevator music on in the background, and the entire place smelled like canned soup.

Not to mention not one of the five people there besides them was under sixty years old.

"Gianni," she said, leaning forward so as not to hurt his feelings.

"I thought you mentioned something about seeing a show tonight. Is it here?"

Please don't be here.

If he was taking her somewhere else, she could beg off and hire a cab to take her home. There was no way she was sitting through anything else with this man. Not now. Not ever.

"Ah, I see, babe, you want some entertainment first, I get it," he snickered loudly, and she blanched.

Whatever he thought was going to happen wasn't. She needed to disabuse him of the notion, and fast.

"Alright, alright. Lemme finish this, babe. Then we'll go up to the room I got for us," he said.

Before she could make sense of the ludicrous statement, he slurped another fried shrimp, don't ask how. Then he grabbed her arm and yanked her from the seat before she could even react.

Elissa tugged on his hold, but the man was immovable. Tossing a five-dollar bill on the table, Little Gianni snatched a toothpick from the hostess stand before dragging her outside.

Great, he was a cheap tipper, too.

All she wanted was to go home. Figuring the best way to do that would probably be to get him to the car, she let him lead the way.

Once inside, she would ask him to drive back to Hoboken so she could wring Gretchen's neck. Fuming, she pulled her arm out of his hand and walked behind him.

The rain was really pouring, and the cheap bastard had refused valet. Elissa ducked her head so she wouldn't get so wet. Of course, the jacket she'd brought was light and had no hood.

Gianni had an umbrella, but he didn't offer to hold it for her, and honestly, she did not relish the idea of getting any closer to him than necessary.

Seriously, not happening.

Now all she had to do was break the news. She had no intention of watching a show or returning to the hotel with him.

What could go wrong?

Grab your copy at https://www.cdgorri.com/books/purrfectly-mated!

EXCERPT FROM BOUND BY AIR

Troy Waman looked down at his smartphone to the little red arrow blinking on his map app, indicating he had reached his destination. He frowned pensively before shaking his head.

"What a fucking shithole," he murmured to himself as he exited the nondescript black SUV his Station Master, Rex, had given him for the job.

"Try not to scratch it," the tough Bear shifter had said with a barely contained growl after their meeting the day before last. After a thousand years of waiting, The *Wardens of Terra* were being called to duty and this was Troy's first assignment.

It took him a day and a half to make his way to Shadowland, New York from the little suburb in Virginia Beach where his Station was located. There were dozens of them across the continental United States and even more overseas, though he'd rarely been out of the county himself.

Troy rolled his shoulders and exhaled. He was the first from his Station to be called to duty. A fact that left him both proud and humbled at the same time. He'd trained damn hard since he was a child waiting for such an opportunity. Now he had it, and it was almost too much to bear.

Fuck and damn. It's time Troy, get your ass in gear. That was all the sympathy he had for himself. Why the hell should he have any at all? Troy Waman was no tenderfoot normal. He was a Warden of Terra. He didn't need to remind himself of the honor and duty that went along with his position.

The *Wardens of Terra* were an ancient group of elite warriors. All of them Shifters. Identified in their youth and trained throughout their preternaturally long lives, they were guardians as well as fighters. *Station Masters* led teams of Wardens across the planet.

Though they'd been deactivated sometime in the last millennium, Wardens were born, chosen, and trained every day with the distinct knowledge that someday, they'd be called upon to defend the earth. That day was here.

Troy Waman had been trained as a Warden since before he learned how to spell the word. His heritage was a mix of Anglo and Native American. His father's blood was a mix of tribes including Algonquin, Lenape, Cherokee, and a few others. He hadn't stuck around long enough for anyone to learn the rest.

He supposed he could get a DNA test, but that might raise too many questions with the normals. Especially in this day of advanced technology in biogenetics.

Besides, it was quite common in today's world to find Native American peoples descended from multiple tribes. Troy Waman was uncommon for an entirely different reason. He was a Shifter, a special race of dual natured beings with one foot in the supernatural world and one in the human. Troy was a *Thunderbird Shifter* to be exact. Something unique even amongst Shifters.

He stretched his long, lithe body as he stepped away from the vehicle. It was already dark out despite it being fairly early in the evening. *Daylight savings my ass.* He sniffed the frigid air. The unusually high winds made the cold seem even more bitter. The street lamp stuttered on the corner, a rusty fence squeaked, and a black cat crossed the street, ducking under some parked cars. Troy's frown deepened.

It looked like the setting of a B-horror flick. All it needed was some half naked co-ed to run down the street with a masked bogeyman stalking behind her, traditional blood-coated knife in hand. *Oh yeah.* They might call it *Shadowland Nightmare* or something equally cheesy.

He stopped his musings and used his heightened senses to take in the downtrodden area around him. It would seem upstate New York wasn't all orchards and sprawling suburbs. He smirked as the "I love New York" song ran through his head. *Yeah, right.*

Apparently, parts of the Empire State were as fucked up as the street where he was born in Newark, New Jersey. He'd visited that shithole back when he was in his teens just out of curiosity. What a mistake that had been! He'd left almost as soon as he'd arrived. His extended family had been, shall we say, less than welcoming.

His gray-haired grandmother had screamed and crossed herself when he stepped over her threshold. He was what they called a *skin walker*. They feared and loathed him as something evil. Him evil? Like he was the motherfucker who knocked-up some unsuspecting normal and left her ass with a Shifter baby.

He was not evil, but he was something they did not understand. He'd been angry and ashamed that day. He'd crashed through his grandmother's kitchen to hitch a ride back down to his Station in Virginia Beach.

In his youth it was more like a military training camp, but it was all he knew of home. After all, it was where he'd lived his entire life. He'd made his peace and settled fully into his life there.

The incident with his grandmother had happened over a decade ago, when Troy had stolen his records out of Rex's office. Still, the memory remained fresh in his mind as if it were only yester-day. The fucked-up street where he was standing only brought back the painful reminder that he'd come from the same kind of squalor. *Fuck this*, he thought.

The pungent scent of despair washed over him. *Reminding him.* A young man with a hood pulled up over his head, eyed him from the street corner. *Drug dealer. Shadowland* indeed. It was an apt name for this shamble of a neigh-borhood.

The young man continued to stare until Troy allowed his beast to shine through. His golden eyes pinned the errant youth through the inky darkness of the night. Startled, the kid dropped the bag he was holding and ran down the alley.

Punk. Troy walked over and picked up what he had so hastily left behind. A couple of grams of crack cocaine and heroin, *probably cut with Fentanyl.* There were also various sized baggies full of what smelled like some below average marijuana and half-rotted psychedelic mushrooms.

Just your garden variety of illegal substances to be found on most street corners in neighborhoods like this one. *Fucking normals.* He frowned and dumped the still sealed contents down the closest storm drain. He sent a quick text to Rex earmarking the location.

Rex would make sure the local police department got an anonymous tip to retrieve the narcotics before someone got hurt. Recreational drug use, mainly the opioid epidemic, was wreaking havoc amongst the humans with more and more of them succumbing to their addictions.

It was troubling, but not Troy's problem. Shifters were extraordinarily hard to kill. Most human drugs had little to no effect on supernatural beings. *Normals,* he growled the thought, *such weak creatures.*

To be fair, Shifters had vices too. He just had little

experience with it. Cecil, a Station-mate of his, had an adrenaline addiction. He was always putting himself in dangerous situations, even during simple training exercises. Fernandez, a Jaguar Shifter, was always trying to get into some chick's pants. *Sex addict.* And he knew of others who channeled their energies into ways he considered to be mostly unproductive.

His opinion, for sure. He'd always been something of a loner by nature. There weren't many Thunderbird Shifters around. Hell, he was the only fucking one he knew of in this part of the world.

He didn't blame or judge his Station-mates for their proclivities. Most of the Shifters he knew had large appetites which included food, exercise, and sex.

Troy had certainly explored that part of him. He wasn't a man-whore or anything, but he'd had his share of women. None of them mattered to him. Just a means to satisfy the occasional itch.

Troy was determined to live his life as a Warden of Terra alone. He never expected to find anyone willing to share what was a potentially deadly existence.

Those who followed the Darkness and evil were always looking for ways to gain the upper hand and it was his job to stop them. The way he saw it, it was an honor and a duty to serve.

He shared this great responsibility with the entire organization. The core belief of the Wardens was based on one indisputable fact Shifters had walked the earth since the dawn of time, even before humankind; therefore, they were responsible for the well-being of the entire planet and all its inhabitants. Especially those who were inherently weaker. Mainly females and *normals*.

There were other supernaturals who believed humans, or normals as they referred to them, were a blight on the planet. Those creatures wished to destroy them and take over.

Demons, Dark Witches, and a whole plethora of evil beings sought the destruction of the normals and the world they lived in. *Idiots! Did they even realize if they destroyed the world, there would be nothing left? Where the fuck would they live?*

Of course, the supernatural world had many agencies that worked towards the common goal of saving the planet. The *Order of the Guardians*, for example, were responsible for policing the various factions of supernaturals.

Shifters generally tended to ally themselves with the Guardians. Sure, there were *bad* Shifters, but he'd never come across any willing to follow the Dark. Simply because most agreed the destruction of the world could not be allowed to happen.

Different Packs and Clans, etcetera, of course, had different ideas. Some wanted to remain secret, others wished to come out, and other still wanted to rule the weaker humans. It was a whole fucking thing, and they argued about regularly.

Troy didn't know from any of that. He spent little time in the human world. His efforts better spent making himself worthy of being a Warden. Training, exercise, and following orders. That's what Troy lived for, it was why he was chosen.

Thunderbird Shifters were very rare. *Special.* He scoffed at the stray thought. But no matter what way he looked at it, Troy was indeed unique. In more ways than one. He was born *marked* by the stars. A *Shifter of Terra.*

From infancy, he was told he carried the power of his sign within him. *Aquarius* ruled his destiny and it would aid him in the never-ending battle against the forces of darkness.

Every single Warden he knew was a Shifter like him. They were the fiercest warriors on the planet. Like many others throughout the last thousand years, Troy, *a Shifter child who was marked,* was taken from his parents and trained by his Station Master until the time when he would be called into use.

All that time, he thought, *and here I am.* He tried to ignore the pressure building inside of him. He felt anxious. His animal pressed against his psyche, comforting him with his presence.

The significance of the moment was not lost on him. The Wardens had waited a millennium to be called to act. *He* had been waiting his entire life.

"Do not fear the future, Troy," the Herald who had visited his Station said to him when he'd brought word that they had been activated, *"Your destiny awaits."*

Troy wondered if the old man referred to the Wardens finally being called to act, or if the elder spoke of yet another legend. Troy had been shocked to say the least when the Herald had entered their tidy little Station in Virginia Beach with his flowing white hair. After he told them the news, he turned to Troy and recited another old tale.

"Young Thunderbird, you are the first to return us to Terra. Do not doubt your worth. Your destiny has been written in the stars since before you were born, Troy Waman. Remember, a Warden discovers his true measure when his fated mate is thrust upon him."

Whatever the fuck that meant. Troy looked down at

his phone, then to the street sign on the corner, and finally, to the faded numbers painted on the mailbox in front of the ramble of a house his map app had brought him to.

Fuck, am I thinking? Fated mates are myths. Stories made up so orphaned Shifters would sleep through the night. He scoffed at the thought. Memories of tales the head nurse, Sr. Maria, had told him at the training camp he'd called home for years invaded his brain.

Memories were pesky things. Sometimes eternal, and always fucking portable. But he was no longer a child. *No more stories, Sister. Now, I act.*

"A thousand years we've waited, and I'm walking into a fucking scene from a bad episode of *Hoarders*," Troy shook his head and frowned at the decrepit house that sat a few hundred feet away from him.

It was cold as fuck outside and his leather jacket did little to warm him. Avian Shifters did not carry around the same bulk as other types of Shifters. He ran hotter than normals, but the single digit temperature froze him to the bone.

True, he wasn't beefy like some of his fellow Shifters, but he was just as incredibly strong, and he was wicked fast. Much stronger than any average male. He paused briefly gauging the atmosphere.

There was something off about the place. He scented *Magic* and something else. His Bird bristled beneath his skin. *Easy now.*

Lightning flashed in the darkened skies, allowing him to see the worn shingles, and cracked siding of the beaten-up colonial in greater detail. More than one window had been smashed and boarded up with cheap plywood.

If anything, it enhanced the creepy haunted house feel of the place. The porch sagged dangerously. He wondered how the place had managed to not be condemned by the town. One thing was certain, it was an ugly little turd of a house.

Who the hell put gray siding on their house anyway? Maybe it wasn't always that color. Maybe the owner liked gray. *Whatever.* He couldn't give two shits about the siding.

His only concern was the increased supernatural activity in the area over the past two weeks. Ever since the owner, a *Mrs. Renalda Curosi*, passed away. *A haunting?*

A creaking sound floated up to his ears and he stilled his movements. The sound developed into more of a *moaning* noise. An unearthly wail. It grew louder as the lightning continued to flash in the sky.

Troy had never seen a ghost. True, there were a

lot of things in the universe he had never seen nor heard of, but that didn't make them any less real.

If ghosts were real, and they made noises, he imagined that pitiful wail was damn close to what it would sound like.

No such thing as ghosts. Yeah, well, most people had never heard of Shifters either. And yet, there he stood.

His Thunderbird shifted once more beneath his skin, the beast flexing his senses as the lightning in the air drew him to the surface. *No.* He told his other half. His human needed to be in control now. He walked across the street, keeping to the shadows.

Something was indeed off about the creepy old house. He inched further to the black door. The knocker was in the shape of a face or mask. No discernible features, just a vague impression of eyes, nose, and mouth. *Shadowland indeed.*

He listened with his enhanced hearing and frowned. There was a distinct voice somewhere beneath the moaning and creaking. A *female* voice. His curiosity was piqued.

From what he'd seen in her file, Mrs. Curosi was ninety-seven when she passed. Her closest living relative was a half-sister, a *Magdelena Kristos,* and she lived over three hours away in New Jersey. The half-sister was cut from Mrs. Curosi's will recently. She'd bequeathed her entire estate, house, bank account, and all her earthly belongings, to someone named *A. Kristos. Another sister? Maybe.*

Troy hadn't given it much thought until now. A crash sounded from inside the house. He perked up as the feminine voice he'd thought he'd heard earlier screamed in pain. *Time to act.*

Grab your copy at https://www.cdgorri.com/books/bound-by-airbooks/bound-by-air!

About the Author

C.D. Gorri is a USA Today Bestselling author of steamy paranormal romance and urban fantasy. She is the creator of the Grazi Kelly Universe.

Join her mailing list here: https://www.cdgorri.com/newsletter

An avid reader with a profound love for books and literature, when she is not writing or taking care of her family, she can usually be found with a book or tablet in hand. C.D. lives in her home state of New Jersey where many of her characters or stories are based. Her tales are fast paced yet detailed with satisfying conclusions.

If you enjoy powerful heroines and loyal heroes who face relatable problems in supernatural settings, journey into the Grazi Kelly Universe today. You will find sassy, curvy heroines and sexy, love-driven heroes who find their HEAs between the pages. Werewolves, Bears, Dragons, Tigers, Witches, Romani, Lynxes, Foxes, Thunderbirds, Vampires, and many more Shifters and supernatural creatures dwell within her worlds. The most important thing is every mate in this universe is fated, loyal, and true lovers always get their happily ever afters.

Want to know how it all began? Enter the Grazi Kelly Universe with Wolf Moon: A Grazi Kelly Novel or pick up Charley's Christmas Wolf and dive into the Macconwood Pack Novel Series today.

For a complete list of C.D. Gorri's books visit her website here:

https://www.cdgorri.com/complete-book-list/

Thank you and happy reading!

del mare alla stella,
    C.D. Gorri

Follow C.D. Gorri here:
    http://www.cdgorri.com
    https://www.facebook.com/Cdgorribooks

https://www.bookbub.com/authors/c-d-gorri

https://twitter.com/cgor22

https://instagram.com/cdgorri/

https://www.goodreads.com/cdgorri

https://www.tiktok.com/@cdgorriauthor

www.ingramcontent.com/pod-product-compliance
Lightning Source LLC
Chambersburg PA
CBHW071218210726
48293CB00002B/482